D0535571

YOUNG SCROOGE

A VERY SCARY CHRISTMAS STORY

R. L. STINE

FEIWEL AND FRIENDS
NEW YORK

A FEIWEL AND FRIENDS BOOK
An Imprint of Macmillan

YOUNG SCROOGE. Copyright © 2016 by R. L. Stine. All rights reserved. Printed in the
United States of America by R. R. Donnelley & Sons Company, Harrisonburg, Virginia.
For information, address Feiwel and Friends, 175 Fifth Avenue, New York, N.Y. 10010.

Our books may be purchased in bulk for promotional, educational, or business use. Please
contact your local bookseller or the Macmillan Corporate and Premium Sales Department
at (800) 221-7945 ext. 5442 or by e-mail at MacmillanSpecialMarkets@macmillan.com.

Library of Congress Cataloging-in-Publication Data:

Names: Stine, R. L., author.
Title: Young Scrooge : a very scary Christmas story / R. L. Stine.
Description: First Edition. | New York : Feiwel and Friends, 2016.
Identifiers: LCCN 2015034643 | ISBN 9781250070159 (hardback) |
    ISBN 9781250112316 (ebook)
Subjects: CYAC: Christmas—Fiction. | Ghosts—Fiction. | BISAC: JUVENILE FICTION /
    Horror & Ghost Stories. | JUVENILE FICTION / Holidays & Celebrations /
    Christmas & Advent.
Classification: LCC PZ7.S86037 Bah 2016 | DDC [Fic]—dc23
LC record available at http://lccn.loc.gov/2015034643

Book design by Eileen Savage
Feiwel and Friends logo designed by Filomena Tuosto
First Edition—2016

10 9 8 7 6 5 4 3 2 1

mackids.com

For Dylan,
Who will never be a Scrooge.

My name is Rick Scroogeman. I'm twelve, and you might say I mainly like to have fun. I like to tease kids and goof with them and give them a hard time and mess with them a little. You know. Just to be funny.

Some kids at my school, Oliver Twist Middle School, call me Sick Rick. Behind my back, of course.

I don't get that.

I think maybe they're jealous because they don't have as good a time in school as I do. Or maybe because I'm bigger than them and more grown-up. I had a growth spurt last summer, and now I'm the tallest one in my grade.

Pauly Stimp, who plays forward on the Twisters

basketball team, only comes up to my chin. Seriously. I call him Stimp the Shrimp.

I'm tall and I'm big. Yeah, I know it looks like I have a big belly hanging over my cargo jeans. But it's all muscle. Go ahead and punch me in the gut. Punch me as hard as you can. You'll see. But be careful—because I punch back. Ha!

Before I go any further, I want to warn you about something. I want to warn you that this is a ghost story.

Maybe you don't believe in ghosts. Or maybe you think ghosts can be friendly and nice, or maybe sad, or maybe they need love, or something icky like that.

That's not what I learned. I learned that ghosts can be *terrifying*. And cold. And cruel. And vicious. And did I mention *terrifying*?

So, that's my warning.

Maybe you thought you were going to get a sweet story about Christmas joy and sparkling snow and good cheer. If that's what you want, go read *Frosty the Snowman*.

Seriously. No one stands around singing Christmas carols all day in the Rick Scroogeman story.

I guess I should also say that I'm afraid of ghosts. But that's the *only* thing I'm afraid of. Don't believe me? Test me. You'll see.

I've been afraid of ghosts since I was a little kid. I saw a dark shadow moving on the kitchen wall. And there was *no one in the kitchen* who could have made that shadow.

Whoa. Creepy, right?

But enough about scary stuff. Being scared is not how I roll.

Here's a good way to get to know me. You can read an essay I wrote for Miss Dorrit's class. She made us all write essays on "What Christmas Means to Me."

Gag me, please.

Yes, it's almost that sick time of year, time for my least favorite holiday. Why do I hate Christmas so much? Well . . . don't just sit there asking questions. Read my essay . . .

WHY I HATE HATE HATE CHRISTMAS
By Rick Scroogeman

I hate hate hate Christmas for two reasons.

One: They make us watch this terrible old movie in school every Christmas. It's called A Christmas Carol, *and it seriously sucks.*

It's about a really old guy who is stingy and grouchy and mean to everybody. And three ghosts come to take him away and show him how mean and rotten he is, and they tell him why he should change and be nice. And why he should like Christmas.

The movie is bad because it's in black and white. Also, the ghosts aren't scary at all. The special effects totally suck. But there's something even worse than that.

The mean old guy is named Ebenezer Scrooge.

Like . . . why?

As everyone knows, my family name is Scroogeman. So every year after we watch this dumb film, the kids in my class think it's a riot to start calling me Scrooge.

Ha-ha. Do I look like I'm laughing? I don't think so.

But that's not the main reason I hate Christmas. I hate it because I was born on December 25. That's right. Christmas Day is also my birthday.

And does anyone ever remember to celebrate my birthday? No way.

They're all too busy putting up lights and decorating the tree and singing carols and getting ready for the Big Day.

Do you know the dumbest thing about Christmas? Decorating a tree. Because you spend hours hanging stuff on the tree. Hours. And then you just have to take it all off. Talk about a waste of time.

Besides, Christmas trees make me sneeze. I'm allergic to them, and I can't breathe when we have a tree in the living room. But does anyone care if I breathe or not? Of course not. It's Christmas.

Because of Christmas, I've never had a birthday party like every other kid I know. I've never been taken to Disney World or someplace cool. I never get to choose what's for dinner on my birthday. We always have to have a Christmas goose. Yuck all. Who eats goose?

And do I get birthday presents like every other kid?

Of course not. I only get Christmas presents. And no one even talks about how old I'm getting and what an awesome guy I am.

See? I get cheated. Cheated out of my birthday every year.

And that's why I say, Bah, Humbug, like the old guy in that movie. And that's why I HATE HATE HATE Christmas.

Can you blame me?

2

Let me tell you. I don't mean to brag, but Oliver Twist Middle School would be dull without me. Ask anyone. And if they say something bad about me, just remember what I said—they're totally jealous.

I hate to say it, but there are a lot of losers in this school. And losers give me a pain.

There's that loser Davey Pittman, leaning over the water fountain. Ever since they showed that Christmas movie yesterday, Davey has been calling me Scrooge. What a fun guy.

Watch me have a little fun with *him*. When Davey bends his head to get a drink, I cup my hands under the water. I fill up my hands—and then I send a big splash of water onto the front of his pants.

Davey makes a gulping sound and steps back, staring down at the big wet spot on his pants.

"Oops," I say, and then I laugh. Ha-ha.

When Davey walks into class, everyone will see the dark spot on the front of his pants and think he had an accident.

Funny, right?

But now Davey is stepping away from the water fountain, red-faced, scowling angrily at me. The kid has no sense of humor. That's *his* problem.

"No hard feelings." I slap him hard on the back. He goes sprawling into the yellow tile wall. "Oops," I say again. What else can I say? Sometimes I don't know my own strength.

The hall is really crowded. Everyone is heading to class. Some kids saw me push Davey Pittman into the wall. They probably think that was mean. They don't realize I was just having fun with him because he called me Scrooge.

I see another friend of mine across the hall, closing up his locker. Jeremy London is a short, pudgy guy with curly blond hair, freckles, and a goofball smile.

He looks frightened when he sees me coming. But we're actually good friends.

"What do you want, Scrooge?" Jeremy asks as soon as I step up to him.

Uh-oh. He shouldn't have said that. I don't think he meant to. But it slipped out of his mouth anyway.

"Would you like a dancing lesson?" I say.

He tries to back away from me, but his locker is in the way. "A dancing lesson?"

"Yeah," I say. And I tromp down on the top of his sneaker as hard as I can with the heel of my shoe.

"Owwwww!" He lets out a cry.

That must hurt.

He starts to hop up and down on one foot.

I clap my hands in rhythm as he hops on one foot. "Dance! Dance! Go, Jeremy! Go, Jeremy!" I shout.

It's so funny to watch him hop like that. I love giving dance lessons. It's one of my favorite jokes.

I wave good-bye to Jeremy and make my way down the hall to Miss Dorrit's class. I have a big smile on my face. I'm thinking about Davey's wet jeans and how embarrassed he looked. And Jeremy hopping up and down like a one-legged kangaroo.

Hey—does anyone have as much fun as I do?

3

In Miss Dorrit's class, I sit on the end in the back row near the window. Lucy Copperfield sits next to me. Lucy is really nice. I've known her since first grade.

Lucy is all about her hair. That's all she cares about. No joke. She has perfect straight black hair parted in the middle and flowing like waterfalls down both sides of her face. She is constantly smoothing down her bangs and running her hands through her hair and making sure it falls perfectly in place.

So whenever I see Lucy, what do I do? I can't help myself. First, I take my thumbs and smear the lenses on her glasses. Then I take both hands and ruffle her hair as hard as I can.

I try to make it stand straight up. I destroy the part and push her hair this way, then that way, until she looks like she has a furry cocker spaniel on her head.

Ha-ha. Funny, right?

Her face turns red and she acts totally annoyed. But I know she thinks it's funny, too.

I look around. No one else is laughing. Am I the only one with a sense of humor in this school?

Lucy shakes her head hard and struggles to smooth her hair into place. "Rick, don't do that again," she says, squinting at me through her smeared glasses.

"Rick, don't do that again," I repeat, imitating her high, squeaky voice.

"Stop it!" she cries. "I mean it!"

"Stop it!" I repeat. "I mean it!" A few kids laugh at my imitation of her shrill little mouse voice.

Lucy raises her hand, trying to get Miss Dorrit's attention. But Miss Dorrit has her back turned, writing on the whiteboard.

"Rick, why are you so juvenile?" Lucy says.

"Ooh. Big word," I say. I slip her phone from her backpack and start pushing things on the keypad.

"Give that back. What are you doing?" Lucy cries. She tries to grab it but I swipe it out of her reach.

"I have to make a call," I tell her. "To China."

"You're not funny," she says through gritted teeth. "Give me back my phone."

"No. Really," I say. "My uncle is in China. One of his business trips. I have to call him." I start pushing numbers on the dial.

"No. Give it back," Lucy cries, grabbing for the phone again. "You can't call China. It will cost hundreds of dollars!"

"That's why I'm doing it on *your* phone," I say.

But, of course, it's a total fake-out. My uncle isn't in China. He's in Cincinnati. And why would I call him in the middle of school?

"Miss Dorrit?" Lucy shouts. "Rick has my phone."

What a snitch.

Up at the front of the room, Miss Dorrit rolls her eyes. "Give her back the phone, Rick," she says. "No phones in class."

I hand Lucy back the phone. "I was only helping her with it, Miss Dorrit," I say. "Her phone had a problem, and I fixed it."

"Liar," Lucy mutters.

I laugh. You have to think fast in school. Most kids don't know how. That's why they're losers.

"Quiet down, people," Miss Dorrit says. That's teacher-talk for shut up.

She's so pretty. She's really young and she has wavy blond hair and amazing green eyes and a funny laugh that sounds like she's hiccupping. She's the most popular teacher in school, at least with the boys.

"Everyone take out a sheet of paper and number it from one to twenty," she says. "We're going to have a quiz on last night's science chapter."

Last night's science chapter? I didn't read it. I had too many TV shows to watch. I had to catch up on a bunch of episodes of *Uncle Grandpa*. I mean, which would *you* choose—your science textbook or Cartoon Network?

In the front row, Josh Cratchit raised his hand. "Does this t-t-t-test c-c-count on our g-grade?" The little mouse-faced wimp has a hilarious stutter.

I raised my hand. "M-M-M-Miss Dorrit?" I asked. "Does the t-t-t-test c-c-count or is it just p-p-p-practice?"

Some kids laughed. I can stutter even better than little Joshy. I saw his face turn bright red.

Miss Dorrit's expression turned angry. "Mister Scroogeman, I'm going to pretend you didn't say that," she said. She always calls you by your last name when she's angry at you. "I think you owe Josh a big apology. And I'm warning you—don't ever do that again."

"S-s-s-sorry," I said.

A lot of kids laughed. Josh turned even redder. He kept his head down. He wouldn't look at me. He should know I was just having fun with him. No hard feelings.

Miss Dorrit opened her mouth to scold me. But the classroom door swung open, and Davey Pittman walked in with the big wet spot on the front of his jeans. "Sorry I'm late," he said.

I could see that everyone was staring at his pants. What a riot.

"What kept you?" Miss Dorrit asked.

Davey pointed at me. "Rick splashed water on the front of my pants."

"Liar," I said. "Davey, you don't have to be embarrassed to tell the truth."

An angry screech escaped his throat. Like a monkey who didn't get his banana.

I had to laugh. It was one of those perfect moments.

Miss Dorrit told Davey to take his seat, and she passed out the quiz questions. "Do your best, everyone," she said. "This is the last quiz before Christmas vacation."

I glanced down the list, and I could see I didn't know any of the answers. I knew what CO_2 was. But what are Au and Li?

That's why I always try to sit next to Lucy. Lucy is very smart and she always does her homework. She gets everything right on Miss Dorrit's quizzes, and she does a very bad job of covering her answers. I mean, she doesn't even try to hide her test paper.

Sweet.

That makes it easy for me to see the right answers, too.

I just lean toward Lucy's desk a little bit and take very quick glances at her paper. Some people might call this cheating. But I think *any* way a person finds the right answers is a good thing. At least you're learning.

I mean, I learned that *Au* stands for "gold" in the periodic table. That was Lucy's answer, and I knew it was right.

I was sailing along, taking quick glances at Lucy's test paper, writing down the right answers. About halfway through the quiz, Miss Dorrit's voice interrupted me. "Lucy? Rick? What exactly is going on, you two?"

I knew I was caught. I had to think fast.

"Lucy has been copying off my paper," I said. "I didn't want to get her in trouble."

Lucy made a choking sound. I slapped her back a few times to help her stop.

"That's not exactly what I saw, Mister Scrooge-man," Miss Dorrit said. "Are you sure you're telling the truth?"

"Pretty sure," I said.

Lucy ran her eyes up and down my test paper. "He copied every one of my answers," she told the teacher.

"Not *every* answer," I said. "I'm only on number nine."

Some kids laughed. But Miss Dorrit didn't crack a smile. "I'll see you in here after school, Rick," she said.

"I can't come," I said. "I have rehearsal for the Christmas play."

"I need to talk to you about that, too," Miss Dorrit said. "Come after school and don't keep me waiting."

"But . . . I'm supposed to give snowman-building lessons to my brother, Charlie," I said. "My mother told me to help him. Charlie doesn't know how to build a snowman, and he needs lessons really bad."

"That's a good one," Miss Dorrit said, rolling her eyes. "I haven't heard that one before."

"Thank you," I said.

"Charlie will have to build his own snowman," she said. "Don't be late."

I took a deep breath. "Does this mean I'm in trouble?"

She didn't answer.

After school, my friends were starting rehearsals for the Christmas play in the auditorium. But I made my way toward Miss Dorrit's classroom.

The hall was nearly empty. Most kids had hurried out into the snow to have fun. It had snowed about six inches the night before, and the snow was fresh and soft and perfect for packing tight wet snowballs.

I love creeping up behind kids and smashing a hard snowball into the back of their head. They never know what hit them. It's such a riot.

Some kids brought their ice skates to school. They planned to go directly to Oxford Pond beyond the elementary school playground to skate. Fun.

I'm a good ice-skater. I love skating really fast and cutting right in front of people, surprising them so they have to come to a sharp stop. Sometimes they lose their balance and fall right on their butt. Ha-ha. They look so funny.

But no fun for me this afternoon. I knew I was heading into a lecture by Miss Dorrit. As I walked, I lowered my head and stared down at the floor and practiced looking sorry for what I had done. Whatever it was.

I turned a corner and—wouldn't you know it—there was Josh Cratchit bending over in front of his open locker, pulling books from the locker floor.

I knew I should walk right past. But I never can resist when it comes to Joshy. With his skinny runt body and his pale face and thick eyeglasses and that horrible stutter, Josh is the perfect victim.

Everyone likes to pick on him. I'm not the only one.

"Josh! Hey—Josh!" I went running over to him. "Be careful!" I cried. "Did you hear? There's an angry pit bull loose in the school."

"Huh?" He turned and his eyes went wide with fright behind his glasses. "A d-d-dog?"

"I'll protect you," I said. I picked him up by his

waist and lifted him into his locker. And then I closed the locker door with him inside.

"Hey—let m-m-me out, Rick!" he shouted.

"You'll be safe now," I said.

Josh was still shouting and pounding on his locker door as I turned the corner and strode quickly down the hall. I knew someone would find him sooner or later.

Sure, I knew that I shouldn't have done it. But Christmas just puts me in such a bad mood. I can't help myself.

Besides, it was pretty funny.

I forced the smile off my face as I stepped into Miss Dorrit's room. She stood behind her desk with her arms crossed in front of her. I guessed she'd been waiting for me.

She was wearing a green sweater that perfectly matched her green eyes. Her blond hair was tied back in a neat ponytail. She had a stern expression on her face. I could see she didn't call me in to give me the Good Citizenship Award.

She pointed to a wooden chair right in front of her desk. "Take a seat, Rick. You and I have to talk." She sat down behind her desk and kept her cold, green-eyed stare on me.

"I have to pick up my brother at the elementary school," I said.

She rolled her eyes. "I know. I know. Snowman lessons."

"No, really—" I said.

"This won't take too long," she replied. She tapped a pencil on the desktop. "How old is your brother, Rick?"

"Charlie is seven," I said.

"Does he look like you?"

"A little," I said. "He has kind of the same face. But he's skinnier than me. He's skinnier than *everybody*. Mom says he looks like a pencil. Totally thin with red hair on top. You know. Like an eraser. I look more like my dad. Dark hair, dark eyes."

"And how do you treat your brother?" she asked.

The question surprised me. "Excuse me?"

"How do you treat your brother?" she repeated. "Are you mean to him? Are you nice to him? Do you stomp really hard on his feet and try to hurt him a lot?"

"No way," I said. "He's my little brother. I'm responsible for him."

She set down the pencil and leaned toward me over her desk. "Responsible for him?"

I nodded. "You know my dad died last year. And Mom . . . well . . . One day she took me aside. And she said, 'You're the man now, Rick. I want you to take care of Charlie. From now on, I want you to look after Charlie and be responsible for him.' "

Miss Dorrit didn't say anything for a long moment. She just kept her eyes on me. She appeared to be thinking hard. "So you don't play tricks on Charlie or push him around or give him a hard time?"

"No," I said. "Well . . . not too often."

That made her smile. But the smile didn't last long. "Did you ever think of treating the other kids you know, the kids here in school, the way you treat Charlie?"

"No," I answered. "Never."

She blinked. "But wouldn't it be better if you treated your friends the way you treat your little brother?"

I shrugged. "I like to have fun," I said. "I like to goof on people. You know. Joke around."

Miss Dorrit tugged at her ponytail. "Rick, what if your brother had a bad stuttering problem?" she said. "Would you make fun of him?"

"My brother doesn't have a stuttering problem," I said.

She sighed. "I know. But what *if*?"

"I don't know," I said. "It's pretty funny to imitate it. I probably couldn't resist."

She narrowed her eyes at me. "You couldn't resist making fun of a stuttering person because . . . ?"

"Because it's funny. I like to be funny and make people laugh. My dad always said I had a good sense of humor."

"But what if your humor makes someone *cry*?" she said.

I shook my head. "I don't get it. Why would someone cry at a joke?"

Miss Dorrit sat back in her seat. She started tapping the pencil on her desk again. "Rick, I don't think I'm getting through to you."

"So can I go?" I started to stand up.

"No. Sit down. We need to finish this. I need to make you understand."

I dropped back onto the chair with a groan. "You want me to apologize to Josh?" I said. "Okay. I'll go get him. I locked him in his locker. I'll go pull him out and apologize."

Miss Dorrit jumped to her feet. "You *what*? You locked him in his locker?"

I nodded. "Yeah. It just kind of happened." I couldn't keep a smile from creeping across my face.

She ran out of the room. I could hear her out in the hall rescuing Josh. When she came back into the room, she was breathing hard.

"This is just what I was talking about," she said. "This is what I'm trying to get you to realize, Rick. A lot of kids don't think you're funny. They think you're really mean."

That word *mean* echoed in my ear.

"Huh, me?" I said. I couldn't keep the surprise from my voice. "Me? Mean? Because I like to kid around?"

Miss Dorrit settled back in her chair. "There are some things you need to learn, Rick. You tried out for a part in Mr. Pickwick's Christmas play, remember?"

"Yes, and I was the best actor there," I said. "The others who tried out were total wimps who muttered onto their chins."

She locked her green eyes on me. "Well, don't you wonder why you didn't get a part? Don't you wonder why Mr. Pickwick made you the stage manager instead of letting you act?"

I returned her stare. "Because he's a jerk?"

She groaned. "Rick, it really isn't a good idea to call your teachers names. Especially in front of another teacher." She shifted in her chair. I don't think she was enjoying our talk. I *know* I wasn't enjoying it.

"Rick, you didn't get a part in the play because the other kids were afraid of you. They were afraid of what you would do to them onstage during rehearsals. They were afraid you would bully them."

"Bully?" I repeated the word.

"We've talked a lot in class this year about bullies," she said. "You remember, don't you?"

I shrugged. "I don't know any bullies," I said. "I think they're probably only in books."

She gazed at the wall clock on the far wall. "I think we have to wrap this up," she said. "But before you go, I just want to say a few more things to you."

She kept talking, but I stopped listening to her. I was thinking hard. My mind was spinning because of what she had told me. The other kids didn't want me to be in the play. That's why I was stage manager.

They didn't want me. They didn't want Rick Scroogeman.

Miss Dorrit was saying something about the Golden Rule. But I didn't hear a word. I could feel the anger bubbling in my chest.

They didn't want me. They didn't want me onstage with them.

Suddenly, I knew what I had to do.

I had to find a way to pay them all back.

And guess what?

I had a really fun idea.

After dinner, Mom, Charlie, and I were in the den. Mom sat on the edge of the soft couch, knitting a Christmas sweater for one of our cousins.

She was always knitting sweaters for our cousins. She never did one for Charlie or me, and I was glad because her sweaters always weigh a ton and they're totally itchy. They itch you right through your shirt. Right through your skin. Seriously.

Mom had the Weather Channel on the TV. She's obsessed with the Weather Channel in winter. She likes all those snowy scenes of cars stranded on the highway and roofs collapsing under six feet of snow. She loves snow disasters.

Mom has a good sense of humor, like me.

Charlie was down on the floor in front of the coffee table. He had a big bag of jelly beans in his lap. I dropped down beside him and swiped the jelly bean bag out of his hand.

"Hey—!" He grabbed for it. Missed.

"Where'd you get these?" I asked.

"Left over from Halloween," he said. "They're mine. Give them back."

"Wow. Look at that car stranded on an icy river," Mom said, pointing at the TV. "How horrible."

"Jelly beans aren't good for you," I told Charlie. "And these are stale."

"Jelly beans don't get stale," he argued. He's very bright for seven. "Give them back."

"Tell you what," I said. "Since I'm a nice guy, I'll share them with you. It's almost my birthday, right? So we can divide them up." I tilted the bag and poured them all onto the rug.

I started making piles. "Two for me, one for you. Three for me, one for you."

He made an ugly face and punched me in the shoulder. He's so skinny and lightweight, I could hardly feel it. "Stop it, Rick. You're cheating!" he whined.

"What are you learning in school?" I asked him.

He thought for a moment. "We're learning about the different states," he said.

"Charlie, tell me what things you learned about the states," I said.

He likes to show off about school stuff. He started to talk about California and then Nevada. Then he moved on to Wyoming.

While he talked, I gobbled up a handful of jelly beans. I figured if I could keep him talking, I could eat most of the candy before he finished.

I ate about two dozen, and I saved him five jelly beans. He *is* my brother, after all.

"Mom, Rick ate my jelly beans," Charlie wailed.

"I shared them with him," I said.

Mom had her eyes on the TV. "Rick, I think I'm going to buy you new snow boots for Christmas," she said.

I almost gagged. "Huh? Boots for Christmas? You're joking, right?"

"He only saved me five," Charlie complained.

I took one out of his hand and ate it.

"You need new boots," Mom said.

"But not for Christmas," I said. "I already gave you my wish list, Mom. Snow boots were *not* on the list. I need the presents I put on the list."

She set down her knitting and turned to me. "I'm a little worried about you, Rick. You had twenty gifts on your list. Why do you think you should get so many?"

"You know why," I snapped. "Because it's my birthday, too. How unlucky is that?" I reached for another jelly bean, but that little pig Charlie had eaten all four of them.

"Most kids have *two* days to get presents," I said. "But because my birthday is December twenty-fifth, I only have one day. It's totally not fair."

"If *he* gets twenty presents, I want twenty presents," Charlie said, crossing his skinny arms over his skinny chest.

"See what a bad influence you are on your brother?" Mom said, frowning at me. "I really think you are being selfish. And you are forgetting the whole meaning of Christmas."

"No, I'm not," I insisted. "The meaning of Christmas is to buy me lots and lots of presents."

"That's not funny," Mom said.

"I'm serious," I said.

"Could I have another bag of jelly beans for Christmas?" Charlie chimed in. "I want a *ton* of presents, just like Rick."

"Do you only think about *getting* presents? What about *giving* presents?" Mom asked me.

"I'm just a kid," I said. "I don't give presents. I only get them."

Mom shook her head. "Rick, you're making me very sad. I think you should go to your room now and think about what the real meaning of Christmas is."

"Okay, okay," I said. I climbed to my feet, pushing my hand down on Charlie's head to help myself up. Then I strode quickly to my room at the end of the hall.

I dropped down on the edge of the bed. But I didn't think about the meaning of Christmas. I pictured those kids who didn't want me to be in the Christmas play. And I thought about *revenge*.

I don't get nervous when I have to speak or read in front of the whole class. I know I'm good at it.

A few mornings later, I strode up to the front of Miss Dorrit's class, swinging my essay at my side. Of course, I tromped really hard on Josh Cratchit's foot as I passed by him.

I couldn't believe how loud he screamed. Who told him to sit with his big foot in the aisle?

Miss Dorrit sat on the edge of her desk. Today she wore faded denim jeans and layers of red and green T-shirts. I stepped up next to her and raised my papers.

"What is the title of your Christmas essay?" she asked.

"My paper is called 'Why I Hate Hate Hate Christmas,'" I answered.

Some kids laughed. I saw Lucy Copperfield roll her eyes. Shamequa Allen, sitting right in front of me, flashed me a thumbs-down.

Miss Dorrit squinted at me. "Is that really what your essay is about?"

"I'm not joking," I said. "I hate Christmas."

"Okay," she replied. "I think we're all a little surprised. But go ahead and read it."

I cleared my throat and started to read. I read about how much I hated the old Christmas movie about Ebenezer Scrooge. And how Christmas is also my birthday, so I get cheated out of a whole day of presents.

The class was totally silent as I read the part about how stupid it is to decorate a Christmas tree. When I finished reading, no one made a sound.

I lowered my paper to my side. Miss Dorrit let out a long whoosh of air. "Well . . . that was certainly *different*, Rick," she said. "Has anyone else written a paper about how much they hate Christmas?"

No hands went up. Of course.

They all wrote sickening papers about waking up Christmas morning, opening their Christmas stockings, and going to visit Granny. I made my way back to my seat in the back row. Josh Cratchit pulled his foot in—but not fast enough. I gave it another good hard stomp as I passed.

Ha-ha. He'll never learn.

"You're totally sick," Lucy Copperfield said as I took my seat next to her.

"Your *face* is making me sick!" I shot back. We always kid each other like that. I took my thumbs and smeared her glasses.

But I had more important things to think about.

The first dress rehearsal of the Christmas play was after school. The first time the actors would be in their costumes. As stage manager, I was in charge of all the costumes and all the props.

It was a big job. And I wanted to make sure I did it right. The Rick Scroogeman way.

Mr. Pickwick, the school drama teacher, met me at the stage door to the auditorium. He's a big guy, in his forties, I think, with a round pink face and long black hair streaked with gray, all curly on his head. I don't think he ever brushes it.

He always has a stubble of black beard on his cheeks, as if he hasn't shaved for a few days. And he wears the same outfit to school every day—baggy khaki pants, a soft white shirt, very wrinkled, and a blue blazer that hangs down nearly to his knees and he never buttons.

Mr. P always seems to have twelve things on his mind at once. He doesn't walk—he darts. I mean, he kind of shoots from one place to another. It's like he's always excited. Like he has too much energy. He looks like someone put him on fast-forward.

He wrote the Christmas play himself. All the songs, too.

I don't think he likes me. Sometimes during rehearsal, I see him watching me from the side of the stage. Like he expects me to do something bad or wrong.

Ha-ha. He's pretty smart.

"Can you help me with these buttons?" Davey Pittman crossed the stage to Mr. Pickwick, holding up both sleeves of his ruffled elf shirt. Davey plays the leader of the elves.

The whole play takes place in Santa's workshop at the North Pole. Santa was run over by a reindeer, and the elves have to take over. They all work day and night to make sure kids will have a wonderful Christmas, even without Santa.

A family from Ohio with five kids arrives at the North Pole. They are looking for Santa Claus. But when they hear what happened to him, they pitch in and work, making toys beside the elves. They say it's their best Christmas ever.

Gag me with a spoon.

How babyish is that?

But . . . some of the jokes are funny, and the songs are pretty good. Especially "The Reindeer Rap," performed by four kids with antlers sticking out of their heads.

Mr. P helped Davey button the sleeves of his elf shirt. I passed out pointy elf shoes to some of the other elves. They were all practicing their tiny elf voices. I waved to Lucy Copperfield. She plays Davey's elf wife. She pretended she didn't see me.

"Mr. P, should I wear the beard today?" the kid who plays Santa asked. He's a fifth-grader named Billy O'Brian. But I call him Belly O'Beast because he's the fattest kid in school. I mean, he totally is a beast.

I like to grab his big belly with both hands, jiggle it up and down, and shout, "Earthquake!" Especially when there are girls watching. Belly's fat face always turns bright red. It's a riot.

I held Belly's red Santa jacket and helped him squeeze into it. Then I fixed the long white wig on top of his head. "You look awesome," I said. "Like a mountain with snow on top." I made sure Mr. P wasn't looking. Then I gave Belly a hard punch in the belly for good luck.

"Places, people! Places!" Mr. P was shouting. "You all look wonderful in your costumes." He motioned with both hands. "Can I get the elves all lined up over here? Where is Mrs. Santa? I need Mrs. Santa stage right."

Debra Davis, who plays Mrs. Santa, was struggling to get her long apron tied behind her back. The strap kept getting caught in the red-and-green vest she wore over her long red dress.

She hobbled toward Mr. P on her high-heeled red shoes. "Mr. P, there's something wrong," she said. She began scratching her side. Then she scratched her shoulder.

The elves were all lined up, Davey Pittman at the front of the line. I saw that they were scratching, too. Davey squirmed as he slapped at the back of his neck. Lucy Copperfield was bending over to scratch her knees. Belly O'Beast pulled off his Santa beard and rubbed his chin and cheeks.

"People? What are you doing?" Mr. P demanded. "What is going on here?"

I watched from the wings. Everyone onstage was

twisting and squirming and scratching. I couldn't keep a big smile from spreading across my face.

"Ants!" an elf shouted. "Look! I'm covered in ants!"

"Me too!" Davey cried. He pulled an ant out of his elf shirt and held it up in front of him. "My sleeves—they're filled with ants!"

The auditorium walls echoed with groans and cries as the kids realized they had ants crawling all over them.

"I—I don't understand!" Mr. P cried.

Some kids were sprawled on their backs, scratching. Others were frantically pulling off their costumes. I saw ants scurry out of the clothes and over the stage. Ants crawled all over Belly's cheeks and forehead.

"I'm covered in ants!" Lucy screamed, twisting and squirming. "Ohh, it itches! It *itches*! Oww! They're *biting* me!"

That made me laugh.

Mr. Pickwick was tearing at his hair with both hands. His eyes were bulging, and his mouth hung open. I think he was in shock.

But then he turned to me, and his expression changed. He blinked a few times. I could see a lightbulb go on above his head. "Rick, the costumes were *your* responsibility," he said, narrowing his eyes at me.

I raised both hands. "I swear I don't know how—"

Belly O'Beast interrupted. "Scroogeman brought a huge ant farm to science class this afternoon."

"Yes, he did," Davey Pittman chimed in. "He was showing off how the ants were building their own city. He said he had at least two thousand ants in the plastic case."

Gulp.

All eyes were on me now. Kids were scratching their arms and legs, scratching the backs of their knees, furiously scratching at their hair. And staring at me.

I couldn't hold it in any longer. I burst out laughing. "Can I help it if some of my ants escaped into the costume cabinet?" I said.

Of course, I was the only one laughing.

"Help me. I can't stop itching!" a girl cried. "I'm going to itch for the rest of my life."

"The ants are biting me! Look. Red splotches all over my arm."

"I'm allergic. My skin is breaking out. Ohhh, I feel sick!"

What a bunch of whiners.

Mr. P walked over to me, an angry scowl on his face. "Rick, why did you do this?" he demanded.

I shrugged. "Because it's funny?"

I didn't want to tell him I did it for revenge. The kids onstage didn't want me to be in the show with them. So I paid them back. A little innocent payback.

No big whoop. Nothing wrong with that—right?

So why did I have to go immediately to the principal's office?

Mr. Martin beckoned me into his inner office with his pointer finger. He doesn't talk much. He's usually quiet and serious. He watches everyone pass by his office through his square-shaped eyeglasses that make his eyes look as big as tennis balls.

But he never says *hi* or *good morning* or *what's up*. Everything about him is serious and quiet. He wears gray suits every day with black or gray ties. His short brown hair is brushed straight back. He smiles sometimes, but I've never seen him laugh. When he talks to you, you have to lean forward. His voice is so soft, his words seem to dribble down his chin.

He pointed to a chair at the end of the table across from his desk. I sat down in front of a laptop computer. He pulled out the chair next to me and sat down.

"I can explain about the ants," I said. "It was a total accident."

Okay, okay. A little white lie.

"I don't want to talk about the ants," he said. I could smell coffee on his breath, kind of sour. His tennis ball eyes stared into mine. "I want to show you a movie, Rick."

A movie?

He started tapping keys on the laptop keyboard. "This is a movie about a boy named Phil," Martin said. "The movie is being shown in schools all over this country because it's about bullying. Do you know what a bully is, Rick?"

I shrugged. "I guess."

"Well, I think you'll recognize what a bully is when you see Phil," he said. A dark screen came up, and he clicked play. "The film is pretty short. When it's over, you and I will talk about it."

He picked some papers off his desk and left the room. I rested my head in my hands and gazed at the laptop screen as the movie began.

I was feeling pretty good. I expected a long lecture about why I shouldn't put ants in kids' costumes and how I ruined the Christmas play. But instead I got to watch a movie.

It was fun, too. The movie was called *Phil's Story*. This guy Phil looked about my age. And like me, he was the biggest kid in his class. He was loud and funny.

In the first scene, he is in the lunchroom. He tries to take a girl's sandwich. When she grabs it back, he tips a whole carton of chocolate milk over her head. She leaves the room screaming and crying. She's your typical bad sport.

Phil goes out on the playground. He takes a Frisbee away from a bunch of little kids and throws it down a sewer. The little kids get all crazy and upset and start crying. They can't take a joke.

A boy and a girl are doing schoolwork together, standing against the wall. Phil sneaks up behind the boy and pulls his pants down. The boy is so embarrassed, he runs away. Then Phil trips a girl carrying a birthday cake to the lunchroom. She falls on top of the cake and crushes it beneath her.

This is a comedy, I thought. *Why is Mr. Martin showing me a comedy?*

Back in school, Phil takes a girl's homework paper away from her. He crosses out her name and puts *his* name at the top. Then he hands it in to the teacher. Very clever.

He presses a finger over one nostril, then blows his nose in a girl's hair. Then he pours a box of grape juice into a boy's backpack.

In the last scene, Phil is taken to the principal's office. The principal is this older woman with a stern expression. She sits him down in front of a laptop. And she shows him a movie. It's called *Phil's Story*.

The movie ended. I gazed up and found Mr. Martin standing behind me. He pulled out a chair and sat across from me. "Rick, do you understand now why we are showing this movie to certain kids across the country?"

"Not really," I said.

My answer made him blink. He clasped his hands together on the tabletop. "Well, do you understand about Phil? Why he has no friends? Why he is so unhappy and alone?"

"Not really," I said. "Phil looked pretty happy to me."

Mr. Martin made a choking sound. He blinked a few times. He pushed his glasses up on his nose. "Well, let me ask you this, Rick," he said in his soft, quiet voice. "What is your opinion of Phil? What do you think of him?"

"He's awesome," I said. "I think he's way cool. I mean, he's the star of his own movie, isn't he? That's totally cool!"

Mr. Martin swept a hand back over his short hair. Behind his thick glasses, his eyes went dead. He had no expression on his face at all. He suddenly looked to me like a balloon the air had all gone out of.

He sighed. "Is there anything about Phil that you would change?" he asked. "Think about it before you answer. Please."

"That striped shirt he wore was kind of lame," I said. "I guess I'd change his shirt."

"You wouldn't change anything about Phil's be-havior?" Mr. Martin raised his voice for the first time. His gray cheeks turned rosy pink.

"Not really," I said.

"You know the costumes for the Christmas play have to be sent to the cleaners now. They won't come back in time. You've ruined the Christmas play for everyone, Rick. How does that make you feel?"

"No big thing. It was kind of funny," I said. "Just a joke, you know?"

"I think . . . I'm going . . . to give up on you . . .

Rick," he said slowly. "I'll have to speak to your mother." He made a waving motion toward the office door. "You can go home now."

"Thank you, Mr. Martin," I said. I climbed to my feet. "And thanks for showing me that movie."

"Please think about Phil later," he called after me. "Think about how Phil should change his behavior."

"No problem," I said. I stepped out into the empty hall. I could hear the kids from the play in the auditorium down the hall. They sounded angry and upset.

I started to the front doors. I pictured them all scratching and squirming with ants crawling up and down their skin. It made me chuckle.

I didn't realize it was the last time I'd ever see my friends. The last time I'd see Mr. Martin. The last time I'd ever see my school.

As I started to walk home that afternoon, I had no way of knowing that my life was about to change, and the terror would soon begin.

"Rick, can you help me?" Charlie greeted me as I came through the kitchen door.

I dropped my backpack on the floor. Then I grabbed both of his ears and tugged them as hard as I could. Charlie has huge ears that stick out like side-view mirrors on a car. I just can't resist them.

"Ow. That hurt." Charlie backed away from me.

"Man up," I said.

Mom stood at the sink, peeling carrots. She turned around. "Don't pull your brother's ears, Rick. We don't want to make them any bigger. How many times do I have to tell you?"

"Five hundred," I said.

"So? Will you help me?" Charlie waved a big sheet of paper in my face. "I need help with my drawing."

"Go help Charlie," Mom said. "Dinner won't be ready for another hour." She squinted at me. "How come you're late? You didn't get into trouble again, did you?"

I shook my head. "No. There was a big insect problem at the Christmas play rehearsal," I said.

Of course, I didn't tell her that I caused the problem.

Charlie grabbed my hand and tugged me to his room. He has an awesome room. Big posters of Thor, the Avengers, the Fantastic Four, and Spider-Man cover the walls.

Charlie is into superheroes and he likes to draw them. The kid has talent. Maybe he'll be a cartoonist someday.

He pulled me to his table and pushed a black marker into my hand. "I'm having trouble drawing a squirrel," he said.

"Huh?" I stared hard at him. "You draw superheroes all the time. You can't draw a simple squirrel?"

"It's for art class," he said. "I'm going to get a grade on it. And I don't know where to start."

"Start with a nut," I said. "Draw a nut. Then draw the squirrel grabbing the nut."

He shoved my shoulder. "Don't be funny, Rick. It has to be good." He pushed my hand toward the paper. "Go ahead. Start it for me. You start it and I'll finish it."

"Okay, okay." I leaned over the paper, pulled the cover off the marker, and started to draw.

It took me less than a minute. I set the marker down, raised the paper, and showed Charlie my drawing.

"Hey! You're dumb!" he cried. "You didn't draw a squirrel. You drew a house."

"I know," I said. "The squirrel is *inside the house*."

I walked out of his room, laughing my head off.

Mom stepped into the hall, brushing her hair back with both hands. "I have to go to the store," she said. "I forgot the chicken broth. I'll be back in twenty minutes. Watch Charlie, okay?"

She didn't wait for an answer. She turned, grabbed her purse, and hurried out the back door.

Perfect. I was hoping she would leave for a while. Because it was time for one of my important Christmas traditions.

I was already having a fun Christmas season. On

Sunday, a group of kids from the high school walked onto our front yard and started singing Christmas carols. They could not *believe* the barrage of snowballs that I heaved at them as they tried to sing. It was a total riot.

Now it was time for another holiday tradition of mine. This was my special tradition where I find where my Christmas presents are hidden, and I check them out before Mom gives them to me.

Ha-ha. Why take chances? In case she messed up, I can give her some new hints about what I need her to buy me. What could be more important at holiday time than getting all the presents I asked for? Especially since it was my birthday, too.

This year, I knew where the presents were hidden. In the big closet up in the attic.

Through the front window, I saw Mom's car speed off. I peeked into Charlie's room to check on him. He was hunched over his squirrel drawing, humming to himself as he drew.

So I crept to the back stairs and climbed to the attic. The wooden stairs were steep and creaky. The air grew hot as I stepped into the attic. It smelled kind of stale up here. A little bit like old sneakers after your feet have sweated in them.

I had to duck my head because the attic ceiling is very low. Gray evening light washed in from the one small window at the other end of the long room.

I unlatched the closet door and pulled it open. A whoosh of hot air greeted me. I fumbled for the light switch and clicked on the single lightbulb that hung on a cord from the low closet ceiling.

There they were. Two piles of Christmas presents stacked against the back wall. One for Charlie and one for me. Already neatly wrapped in shiny red-and-green-and-silver paper.

I walked over to them and counted. Eight presents for me. Six for Charlie. Not bad.

But the big question was, did I get the PlayStation games I wanted? Or did Mom blow it and buy me baby games again this year? Or Xbox games that don't work on my player?

I had to find out. I grabbed the present on top of my pile and ripped open the wrapping. *Yes!* One of the games I asked for. I tore off the wrapping on the next present. *Oh, wow.* A gross, ugly sweater. What is her problem? I *told* her not to buy me clothes.

I tossed the sweater to the floor and grabbed the next present.

I realized I was sweating. Was it that hot in the closet? Or was I just excited about seeing my presents?

I tore off the wrapping. Handkerchiefs? Huh? A whole bunch of handkerchiefs. Was she out of her mind?

The next present was just as lame. A hairbrush. Yuck.

Mom was totally blowing it this year.

I unwrapped the next one on the pile. Whoa. *A Christmas Carol* songbook. Kill me now.

Worst. Presents. Ever.

The others were a little better. I finished checking them out. Then I rewrapped them quickly. Too bad that I was so eager, I ripped a lot of the paper.

I started in on Charlie's presents next. I had to make sure he didn't get anything that I wanted for myself.

I was about halfway through his presents. Looking at a paint set the little kid was sure to go nuts over. Ha-ha. Another ugly sweater. He'll *hate* it.

I stopped when I heard a sound.

A creak. A quiet squeak.

I glanced up in time to see the closet door start to swing closed.

"Hey!" I cried out. "Who's there? Charlie? Is that you?"

The door shut with a hard slam. I heard a click. The latch on the other side of the door.

"Hey!" I called out again. I dropped the sweater to the floor and lurched to the closet door.

I gave it a hard push. It wouldn't budge. I pushed again. Again. Oh, wow. I was locked in.

"Charlie—open up!" I shouted. "You're not funny. Open the door if you don't want to get pounded!"

Silence.

"You're dead meat, Charlie!" I screamed. "Open this door! Charlie?"

I pressed my ear against the closet door and listened. Silent out there. No creaks. No footsteps. No one breathing hard.

He wasn't there.

I was trapped in the closet. My heart was pounding now. Drops of sweat dripped down my forehead and cheeks.

I tried the door again. No. I couldn't move it.

Then the lightbulb went out.

And it got really scary.

I froze there with my shoulder against the closet door. I blinked in the deep darkness.

"Whoa," I muttered to myself. The closet suddenly felt hotter, as if someone had turned up the heat. I sucked in a deep breath, and the air burned my throat.

Locked in a pitch-black closet, and no one knew I was up here.

I mopped sweat off my forehead with one arm. My *hair* was wet and sweaty. I made a wheezing sound as I sucked in another breath.

No air in here, I thought. *It's getting hard to breathe.*

That thought sent a chill of panic shooting down my body.

I reached for the light switch. Clicked it several times. No light. The bulb was definitely burned out.

Should I call for help? Will Charlie hear me downstairs?

It was worth a try. I opened my mouth to shout. But I stopped when I saw an eerie green-yellow mist swirling at the other end of the closet.

I uttered a sharp gasp. It looked like a cloud. It curled in on itself like a snake. I stared without breathing, without moving as the mist curled and uncurled, up to the closet ceiling, then down again, floating closer . . . closer to me.

Was it going to wrap itself around me?

"Nooooo!" A cry escaped my throat.

The mist grew brighter. The green faded as the yellow flamed. Sparks spit out from the swirling serpent of fog.

"What is happening?" I choked out in a whisper.

The air suddenly felt cold, cold and heavy and wet.

The mist rose up in front of me. It formed a glowing, yellow wall. So bright I had to shut my eyes.

I was shivering now. Shivering from the cold and from my fear.

And when I opened my eyes, I found myself staring at a face.

A pale yellow face. An old man's face, with scraggly white hairs on a craggy bald head, white whiskers down both cheeks. His nose came to a sharp point. His eyes glowed red like burning coals. He wore a gray nightshirt down to his knees. It hung loosely on his thin body.

I couldn't look away from the glowing red eyes. They held me as if I were hypnotized.

And then I suddenly realized what had happened. The closet was so warm. I had fallen asleep. I had drifted off to sleep, and now I was having a nightmare.

"Am I dreaming this?" The words escaped my throat in a hoarse, trembling voice. "Can I wake up now?"

"You're not dreaming," the old man replied. The words sounded as if they were coming from somewhere far away, not from this glowing yellow figure in front of me.

I swallowed. My mouth was dry as sandpaper. I started to shake.

I told you, there's only one thing in this world that I'm afraid of, and that's ghosts. And now I knew I was staring at a ghost. I was locked in this closet with a terrifying ghost.

"Wh-who are you?" I cried in a tiny voice.

"Don't you recognize me?" he boomed. The bright, pulsing light billowed around him.

"N-no," I stammered. "Why should I recognize you?"

A wave of heat washed over me. The old ghost's eyes bulged. "I'm Marley's ghost," he shouted, his voice echoing in the tiny closet.

My mouth dropped open. "Huh?"

His eyes narrowed on me angrily. "I'm Marley's ghost. I've come to warn you, William Delaney."

"Whoa." I raised both hands, signaling him to back off. My brain spun with confusion. "William Delaney?" I choked out.

The old ghost raised a bony finger and pointed. "You are William Delaney. Don't try to escape your fate, William. You cannot run from your doom."

"But—But—" I sputtered. "I'm not William Delaney. I'm Rick Scroogeman."

A flash of light made me blink. The ghost appeared to fade for a moment. He slipped back in the darkness of the closet until he appeared dim and small. "Scroogeman?" he said. "You're telling the truth?"

I let out a long, shuddering breath. "The Delaneys live across the street," I said. "The redbrick house on the corner. You got the wrong house."

Marley's ghost nodded slowly. His eyes appeared to sink deep in their sockets. A low hum came from deep in his chest. "Sorry about that," he said. He turned to the wall. "I'll be gone now. I have to haunt William Delaney."

"Uh . . . wait," I said. "Before you go, could you do me a favor? Could you open the closet door for me and let me out?"

He had nearly disappeared. Only his face and one hand remained, floating in front of me.

He floated closer, his ghostly face just inches away. "Your turn is coming, Scroogeman. You must remain in this closet. Your journey is about to begin."

"You won't help me?"

He didn't answer. He lowered his head and began to vanish through the wall.

"Don't let the door hit you on your way out," I said.

He was gone. Marley's ghost was gone. I sat there, still shaking, staring at the glowing darkness where he had floated.

Then the darkness exploded into bursting red and yellow lights. And from the flash of light came a deep voice: "I've come for you, Scroogeman. I've come for you now."

10

The bright colors faded. Blinking hard, I waited for my eyes to adjust to the dim light. And stared at a hooded figure. His long gray robe reached the floor, covering his whole body. It billowed like drapes at an open window, and I heard a sound like rushing wind.

I couldn't see his face. It was hidden under the hood. "I've come for you, Scroogeman," he repeated in his deep bass drum of a voice.

He turned toward me and I could see into the hood. I saw only blackness in there. No face. No face at all.

"G-go away," I stammered. "You have the wrong guy. You want Delaney across the street."

"I want *you*," the ghost boomed. And again I heard

the wind, as if a storm had blown up inside his empty hood.

"Wh-what do you want?" I choked out. "This isn't Halloween. You're too late for the costume contest."

The wind became a roar, like a powerful burst of thunder. I fell back against the closet wall. My whole body shuddered.

"I am the Ghost of Christmas Past!" the hooded figure screamed.

"You don't have to shout. I can hear you," I said, rubbing my throbbing ears. I stared into the hood, into the solid blackness.

"I am the Ghost of Christmas Past," he repeated, a little softer.

"And I'm the Easter Bunny," I said. I don't know where I got the courage. But my fear turned quickly to anger. "Get out of my closet. Let me go."

The ghost floated over me. "You'd better act more scared," he warned. "I really am a ghost."

And now I started to shudder. Sitting on the floor with my legs outstretched, my knees began to knock. I couldn't stop them.

I told you before, I've been afraid of ghosts my whole life. Ghosts are the only thing I'm afraid of.

And now here I was, locked in the attic closet,

storm winds blowing, and a headless, hooded ghost come to haunt me.

"What do you want? Where are you taking me?" I cried.

But he didn't answer my question.

"Scroogeman, you have ruined Christmas for the kids in the school play," he said. "You have frightened your classmates and made their lives unhappy. And now you have ruined Christmas for your mother and your brother by tearing up all the presents."

An invisible hand clamped onto my shoulder. I couldn't see it, but it felt wet and cold. "Come with me. I'm going to take you to where you can see the error of your ways."

He tightened his hold on me until I gasped in pain. "Is this like the movie?" I cried. "That gross Christmas movie—?"

"IT ISN'T A MOVIE!" he boomed, his voice rattling the closet door. "This is real, Scroogeman."

The wind picked up again. It quickly grew to a roar. And then a *deafening explosion* rocked the closet. I covered both ears with my hands as the blast sent me flying off the floor.

Flying into a deep blackness.

I could still feel the bone-hard grip of the ghost's invisible hand pulling me. I couldn't see him. I couldn't see anything. But I felt him pulling me away . . . away from the closet . . . away from my home.

Pulling me . . . away.

11

I shut my eyes tight. Swirling winds howled around me. I heard voices moaning as if in pain. I heard loud sobs. Someone groaned, "*Help me . . . Hellllp me . . .*"

The cries made me open my eyes. No one there. I was still being pulled through total darkness. The skin tightened on my face. I couldn't breathe. The wind was smothering me.

Was that *me* screaming? Wailing at the top of my lungs without stop?

My cries echoed as if I were in a huge cave. And then . . . I was on a street corner. The hooded ghost stood beside me, still squeezing my hand in his icy grip.

Too dizzy to stand, I slumped onto my knees. My

head felt like a spinning top. The ground tilted and swayed.

Finally, I felt a little stronger. My heart pounding, I climbed to my feet. I was suddenly wearing a heavy overcoat and a fur hat I'd never seen before.

I gazed around. A tall, dappled horse clopped past, pulling a small wooden carriage. No cars on the street.

Two men walked past, wearing long black overcoats and wide-brimmed hats pulled down low over their heads. They stepped over snowdrifts, their leather boots nearly up to their knees. One of them carried a slender silver walking stick. He gestured with it in the air as he talked.

Two men on horseback trotted past. And then another horse-drawn carriage.

"Where am I?" I demanded. My voice came out faint and shrill, like a whistle. "Is this the past or something?"

The ghost nodded. "You got that right."

Two women wearing big gray bonnets and fur-collared coats over long, pleated skirts walked past. One of them walked right *through* the ghost!

That sent a chill down my back. He wasn't kidding about the ghost part.

That meant I'd been kidnapped. Kidnapped by a

crazy invisible ghost and taken . . . taken who knows where!

Were there police here? Could I report him to the police? Can you report a *ghost* to the police?

I suddenly thought about Charlie. Mom was at the store. He was home all alone. What if I couldn't get back home? Did that mean he'd get all of *my* presents, too?

No way I'd let that happen!

I tugged my hand free from the ghost's cold grip. "You have to take me home," I said.

"No, I don't," he said. "I have taken you far from your home. To a distant time. Before you were born."

"But my mom will be waiting. She—"

"Your mother hasn't even been born yet," he said. "Scroogeman, I brought you back to the distant past to show you a lot of things. You ruined Christmas for a lot of people. Now you need to learn the real meaning of the holiday."

"But I already know that," I protested. "What do you think I was doing in that attic closet? I was discovering what's important about Christmas—my presents."

He shook his head. Two tall dark-hatted men in long overcoats walked past, both rubbing their beards and talking at once. One of them walked through the ghost as if he were made of air. The ghost didn't seem to mind.

I'm the only one who can see him, I realized.

No way I could report him to the police.

"Wh-why did you do this to me?" I stammered. "Why did you bring me so far back in the past?"

He lowered his hood close to my face. I could still see only darkness inside. "Because I knew you wouldn't like it," he whispered.

The answer sent a chill down my back. "But . . . in the movie, the Ghost of Christmas Past makes Scrooge revisit his childhood," I said.

"This isn't a movie," he snapped. "You have many lessons to learn, Scroogeman. You need to learn how to treat the people you know. Have you ever heard of the Golden Rule?"

"Sure," I said. "Do it to others before they do it to you."

He remained silent for a long time. "Okay," he said finally. The gray hood bobbed up and down. "Okay. That's the Golden Rule. I have brought you back in time to a place where they practice *your* Golden Rule."

"Good," I said. My head was spinning. I didn't really know how to reply.

" 'Do it to others before they do it to you,' " the ghost repeated. "Let's see how you like that, Scrooge-man."

The long robe swirled around him as he turned away from me. He floated into the street as a horse and carriage clattered by.

"Hey, wait!" I called. "Where are you going? You can't just leave me here. Where are you going?"

He turned, and again I saw the empty blackness inside the hood. "Time for you to start school, Scrooge-man. Follow me."

12

Everything went black. When I could see again, we were standing in a dimly lit hall. Torches along the wooden wall provided a flickering light. Christmas wreaths were hung at the windows. Weird-looking, old-fashioned-type kids carrying leather book bags by their straps strode past us.

"This is your new school, Scroogeman," the Ghost of Christmas Past said. "The Bleak Academy."

I stared at the kids walking past. Some of the boys must have been farmers. They wore dark denim overalls to school. Flannel shirts and bib overalls with straps like suspenders.

Totally weird.

The girls had hair down to their shoulders, tied back in colored ribbons. They all wore long skirts, gray or black, that came down to their heavy leather shoes.

Everyone talked quietly, like they were afraid to make any noise. The loudest sound was the clump of their heavy shoes on the wooden floor.

"I don't want to go to this weirdo school. I want to go to my own school," I told the ghost.

"Your mean nature has brought you here, Scrooge," the ghost said. His robe shimmered in the flickering torchlight. "Let us see how you enjoy being in a school where everyone treats you the way you treat others."

" 'Mean nature'?" I cried. "Who says I'm mean? Tell me. Who said it? I'll punch out his lights."

He didn't reply.

"Take me home!" I demanded. "I don't belong here." I grabbed for his arm, but my hand went right through the sleeve of his robe. "You can't do this to me. I'm not going to move until you take me home. Do you hear me?"

"Good luck in your new school, Scroogeman," he said softly. "You'll need it."

Then he vanished in an explosion of cold air.

And I was left standing there in that dark hall, in

my jeans and blue polo shirt, the only kid not dressed in gray or black. The only guy in the school with short hair. The only guy here who didn't know anyone at all.

"I DON'T BELONG HERE!" I wanted to scream at the top of my lungs.

Would anyone care?

A tall, skinny boy in a wrinkled gray shirt tucked into his overalls stepped beside me. He swept back the straight brown hair that had fallen over his forehead. He had little round brown eyes and a long nose that came down almost to his lips.

He looked a lot like a bird. If I'd been back home, I'd have offered him a worm. Ha-ha.

He squinted at me for a long moment. "Are you the new boy?"

I nodded. "I guess."

"You're Scroogeman?" he asked, still studying me.

I nodded again. "I guess."

"I'm Benjamin Cooke," he said. "Mr. Dulwich asked me to watch for you."

"Who is Mr. Dulwich?" I asked.

"Our teacher," he said. He squeezed the sleeve of my polo shirt. "Your shirt is the color of the sky," he said softly.

"So what?" I said.

"Did your mother dye it that color when she wove it for you?" he asked.

I started to tell him my mom bought it at Walmart. But another boy walked up to us. He was big and red-faced and blond and bounced as he walked. He had a black tie knotted at the stiff white collar of his white dress shirt. He grinned at me. "New boy?"

"Watch out for Prescott," Benjamin whispered in my ear. He took a step back.

"Yeah. I'm new," I said. "You're Prescott?"

"We don't like new kids," he said. "I already don't like *you*. Why are you wearing a circus costume?"

"Why are you wearing *that*?" I said, pointing to his heavy brown suit jacket and vest. "Do you have a monkey at home waiting to get his suit back?"

I thought it was pretty funny, but Benjamin and Prescott didn't laugh. Prescott's face turned red and he clenched his fists. "No one makes a monkey out of me," he said through gritted teeth.

I decided I'd better not get him steamed. It was my first day, after all. "I was making a joke," I said.

"Your *mother* made a joke," Prescott said. "I'm staring at it."

Benjamin laughed at that one. I decided to play it cool. I didn't say anything about *his* mother.

Some kids had gathered across the hall to watch us. I spotted a very hot-looking girl with long, wavy blond hair down the back of her gray dress. I flashed her a thumbs-up. She turned her head away.

"What are *those?*" Prescott asked. I realized he was staring down at my sneakers. "Why are you wearing *cloth* on your feet? Are you an elf who lives in the forest?"

"Those are Air Jordans," I said.

He scowled at me. "Elf Jordans? You think you're a forest elf?"

"No. *Air* Jordans," I repeated.

"What kind of cobbler would make shoes out of cloth?" Prescott asked Benjamin.

Benjamin shrugged. "Maybe a *blind* cobbler?"

They both thought that was a riot. They tossed back their heads and laughed.

"That's not funny," I said. "These sneakers cost my mom a lot of money."

"I'll show you what's funny," Prescott said, winking at Benjamin. "Let me test those elf shoes."

He raised his big boot and tromped his heel down as hard as he could on the top of my right sneaker.

"Whooooa." I let out a howl of pain.

"*That's* funny!" Prescott exclaimed. He slammed his heel down hard again on the same spot.

"I see . . . what . . . you're doing," I choked out as pain shot up my leg, up my entire body. "You're . . . giving me . . . a dance lesson."

The pain was unbearable. I shut my eyes and started to dance.

13

Mr. Dulwich was tall and skinny as a spaghetti noodle. He had straight black hair parted in the middle of his head. And he wore round eyeglasses perched on the end of his long nose.

His shirt collar was stiff and stuck out like wings. It wasn't even attached to his starched white shirt. A black string tie hung down from his neck. His suit was black. The jacket was tight against his waist, and the pants were baggy.

I'm not the one dressed like a clown, I thought. *Put a red nose on Mr. Dulwich and he could perform in any circus.*

He greeted me with a short hello. Then, with a

wave of his hand, he sent me to an empty desk-chair at the back of the room. I had to squeeze into it. The chair was pretty small.

I turned and saw the blond girl from the hall sitting next to me. She had awesome blue-gray eyes and a few freckles on her cheeks. She didn't say hello or anything. She was busy arranging black pencils in a wooden pencil box.

"Hey," I said. "How's it going?"

She finally looked at me. "How's *what* going?" she asked.

I flashed her my best smile. "How you doing?"

"How am I doing *what*?" she demanded.

"Just saying hi," I said. "What's your name?"

She tossed back her hair. "Emily-Ann. May I ask a question? Why are you wearing such funny clothes?"

"Because I come from the future," I said.

She laughed and turned back to her pencil box.

"We have a new student, class," Mr. Dulwich announced. He stood at the front of the room, leaning on an enormous globe of the world. "Stand up and introduce yourself," he said, motioning to me with both hands.

It took a struggle to climb up from the little desk-chair. "I . . . I'm Rick Scroogeman," I said.

"Rick *Stoogeman*," I heard a boy in the front row say. I recognized him. Prescott.

Most everyone laughed. Then they began to chant. "Stoogeman! Stoogeman! Stoogeman!"

Dulwich raised both hands to get them quiet. "And where do you come from, Rick?" he asked.

"Rockford," I said. "It's a little town in Illinois."

He squinted at me. "Indian country? You come to us from Indian country?"

"That's why he's wearing moccasins!" Benjamin chimed in.

"He's an Indian from the Stoogeman tribe!" Prescott declared.

And they started to chant again. "Stoogeman! Stoogeman! Stoogeman!"

How annoying is that?

Next to me, Emily-Ann was chanting louder than anyone and laughing. Enjoying it too much.

On an impulse, I grabbed the back of her hair and gave it a tug. You know. Playful. Not too hard.

Her eyes went wide in surprise. Then she opened the lid to her desk, pulled out a small black bottle, and emptied it over my head.

It didn't take me long to realize it was black ink. It oozed down my hair and down both sides of my face.

That stopped the chanting. Everyone turned to stare.

Mr. Dulwich came striding down the aisle and stopped in front of Emily-Ann's desk. "That is no way to greet a new student," he scolded her.

"But it was an accident!" she cried. "My hand slipped, sir."

A lot of kids laughed.

I felt like a total jerk, sitting there with black ink running down my hair and face. But I was impressed with Emily-Ann. She was a good liar, maybe as good as me.

"Mr. Scroogeman, you will find some towels in the housekeeping cupboard," Dulwich said. "Dry yourself as best you can." He turned to the class. "The rest of you, take out your chapbooks. We shall have some quiet reading."

"Don't you mean Chap*stick?*" I said.

He frowned at me. "Was that meant to be a joke? I'm sure I don't understand it."

The other kids were pulling these little books from their desks. The books didn't seem to have covers. Just pages.

I climbed out of the tiny desk-chair and started up the aisle to the classroom door. The ink smelled sour, and I could feel it drying in my hair. I wondered where the boys' room was. Maybe this horrible school didn't even have one.

I was nearly to the front of the room when Prescott stuck his foot out and tripped me. I stumbled into the big globe. Landed on top of it. And the globe and I rolled across the floor.

I finally managed to climb to my feet, and I set the globe back on its wooden stand. The whole class was howling with laughter. Prescott was laughing harder than anyone. He stared at me as if challenging me.

Challenging me to a fight?

I ignored them all and made my way into the narrow, dimly lit hall in search of the cupboard with the towels.

I knew what was going on here. I knew it was payback time for me. That hooded ghost wanted to teach me a lesson. He knew my new classmates would play the same kind of jokes on me that I play on others.

I got it. I'm not stupid.

The question was, what was I going to do about it?

The answer came to me instantly. I was going to tell the truth to these kids. Explain to them who I really am. And ask them to help me get *out* of here.

14

After school, I tugged on my heavy overcoat and followed the others outside. I saw Benjamin, Prescott, and Emily-Ann walking together along a narrow path cut into the deep snow. The bare trees rattled in a cold wind. The three kids wore long overcoats buttoned to the collar. Their heavy shoes crunched on the hard snow.

I called to them. "Wait up!"

They turned, shifting the straps of their leather book bags. "It's the Stoogeman," Prescott said, grinning.

I ran up to them, slipping on the icy ground. "Are you walking home?" I asked.

"We take a shortcut through the woods," Emily-Ann said.

"Can I talk to you for a minute?" I asked.

Prescott rolled his eyes. We were standing in the shadow of a low, flat-roofed shed behind the school. It smelled really bad. I realized it was the school bathroom.

Large blackbirds pecked at the ground all around us. Even though the afternoon sun was still high in the sky, a pale white sliver of a moon appeared low over the bare trees.

"What do you want, Stoogeman?" Benjamin asked. He reached out and mussed up my hair with his hand. Then he turned to Emily-Ann. "Think that ink will ever come out?"

"Probably not," she said.

"That was a tragic accident," Prescott said. All three of them burst out laughing.

"Can I have your moccasins?" Benjamin asked, pointing at them. "I've always wanted real Indian moccasins."

"They're not moccasins, "I said. "They're Air Jordans. Sneakers. I told you."

"They might fit me," Benjamin said. "Give them to me."

"No way," I said.

"Give them to me and you can be my best friend," he said. That made the other two laugh.

"Listen, I know what you're doing," I said. "This is the kind of thing I do to kids back home. But please . . . you've got to help me."

"Help you out of your moccasins?" Benjamin said. He grabbed my leg and started to reach for my shoe.

"No. Wait. Please."

If it came to a fight, I could probably take Benjamin, I thought. *But Prescott is too big. He'll flatten me.*"

"I need help," I said. "You see, I don't belong here."

Prescott rolled his eyes again. "We've been trying to tell you that."

"No," I said. "You don't understand. I don't live here. I come from the future. See how I'm dressed? That's how we dress in the future."

"Too bad," Emily-Ann muttered.

"People dress in funny colors in the future?" Prescott asked. "And wear cloth elf shoes?"

I nodded. "You probably don't believe me," I said, "but—"

"That's the smartest thing you've said," Benjamin interrupted. "We don't believe you."

"How can I convince you?" I said. "I'll tell you some other things we wear. We wear a lot of T-shirts."

Emily-Ann squinted at me. "Shirts to wear to tea? Why would you wear a special shirt to tea?"

I let out a long sigh. I realized I wasn't getting any-where with these kids. All three of them stared at me with tight grins on their faces. Of course, they believed I was crazy.

I took a deep breath and tried again. "I really need your help," I said. "I know it's hard to believe, but I don't live in your time. I live in the twenty-first century."

"And do you come from up *there?*" Prescott said. He pointed up to the moon. All three of them laughed.

"That explains why you are so strange," Emily-Ann said. "You come from the moon. We should have guessed it. And are you going to fly back up to the moon for dinner tonight?"

"He's a Moon Man. He flies home to the moon every night," Benjamin said. "That's why we've never seen him in the village."

"Where do you live?" Emily-Ann asked.

"I . . . I don't know," I answered.

They laughed again.

Where *did* I live? The ghost never told me. Maybe I didn't have a place to live. Maybe he wanted me to freeze to death in the snow.

"Please—" I begged. I know, I know. I never begged for anything in my life. Other kids begged *me* for things. But I couldn't help it. I was desperate. "Please. You don't have to believe me. But I need you to help me."

"Remember that crazy book I read?" Emily-Ann said to Prescott. "It was a story about how they made an enormous cannon and shot three men to the moon. Mr. Dulwich said he read it, too."

Prescott slapped me on the back. "Okay, Stooge-man. We'll find a big gun and shoot you to the moon."

"Stop it," I said. "I told you, I don't live on the moon. I live in Illinois. In the twenty-first century."

"Do you have a fever?" Benjamin asked. "You could see Dr. Honeycutt in the village."

I sighed again. "I guess you can't help me. I just thought maybe you could tell me how to get away from here. Maybe get to a big city. Maybe . . ." My voice trailed off.

I was trapped back in the 1800s. I suddenly thought about Charlie. And Mom. Were they looking for me? Were they worried to death because I had disappeared?

Would I ever see them again?

And what about my Christmas presents? What would Mom do with them if I wasn't there?

I almost had tears in my eyes. I'd never felt so sad in my life.

"I can help you," Prescott said, breaking into my frightening thoughts.

I blinked. "You can?"

"Time travel," he said. "That's what you want. Time travel, like in one of those crazy novels."

I nodded. "Yes. That's it. That's what I need."

Emily-Ann and Benjamin exchanged glances. Prescott kept his eyes on me. "I can help you with that," he said. "Meet me right here tonight after dinner."

15

That night, I waited for Prescott on the path behind the school. Even in the heavy overcoat, I hugged myself against the cold blasts of wind that sent swirls of snow flying all around. The pale moon was high in the sky now, and the wintry bare trees rattled and shook as if they were shivering, too.

My teeth were chattering by the time Prescott arrived, tromping over the deep snow in his knee boots. He was followed by Emily-Ann and Benjamin, both wearing tall fur hats, their heads down, bending into the wind. Silvery light washed down over all of us. No other light anywhere.

I felt as if I were walking in a dream, a dream of

silver light and purple shadows. I kept waiting for the ghost to appear. I kept thinking he would come and ask me if I'd learned my lesson about the Golden Rule. And I'd say, "Yes, of course, I have. I have learned a lot and I'm ready to go home."

Maybe that was a lie. But in my daydream, the ghost believed me and instantly took me home.

Daydreams usually don't come true. The ghost was nowhere to be seen. And here I was, shivering in the dark, squinting at the three kids in their black over-coats and fur hats. Desperate for them to help me.

"Do you really know something about time travel?" I asked Prescott.

He nodded. "I do. We're going to take you to the time tunnel, Scroogeman. We're going to send you home."

My chest suddenly felt tight. My heart began pounding. Should I believe him?

I had to. I had to believe he really knew how to send me back where I belonged.

The other two kids didn't say a word. They kept their heads down. When they raised them, I saw the solemn expressions on their faces.

This was serious stuff. No kidding around.

For a moment, I felt like leaping up in the air and cheering. I had the urge to bump knuckles with all three of my new friends. But, of course, that would only confuse them. No one bumped knuckles in this time. They didn't seem to touch at all.

"Follow me," Prescott said, his voice just above a whisper.

We started to follow the path. No one spoke. The only sounds were the rattling of the trees, the howls of the swirling winds, and the crunch of our shoes on the snow.

The path cut through a patch of trees and then over a wide, flat clearing. In the distance, I saw a small farmhouse, flickering orange light in one window. It vanished in the darkness as we kept moving.

How far did we walk? I can't tell you. My brain was spinning with thoughts about time travel and returning home.

We came to a snow-covered rail fence and stopped. "Climb over," Prescott instructed me. "This is Morgan's farm. The time-travel tunnel is here. But no one ever dares go near it. Everyone in the village is afraid."

My heart started to pound even harder. I knew I was close now.

I gripped the top rail and hoisted myself over the fence. The other three followed. As we started to walk again, a long, low building came into view, black against the gray-black sky. The building clung to the ground like a tunnel, and I knew this was it. This was my way home.

I was breathing hard as we stepped up to one end of the long building. I could see a wooden doorway with crisscross slats in the center of the wall.

"This is the tunnel through time," Prescott said in a whisper. I could barely hear him above the rush of the wind.

"Good luck," Emily-Ann murmured. Benjamin remained silent. He hung back as if he were afraid to come too close.

"You need to take a running start," Prescott instructed me. "Lower your head and run full speed. I'll swing the door open. Don't stop. Run as hard as you can."

I nodded. "I will," I said, my voice trembling. "Thank you. Thank you all for bringing me here."

Prescott placed a hand on my shoulder. "We wanted to send you where you belong," he said. "Now go. Go fast."

He strode to the wide wooden door and signaled for me to run.

I took a deep, shuddering breath. Lowered my head. And forced my legs to move. The door swung open and I ran into the blackness of the tunnel. Ran faster than I'd ever run in my life.

16

As I stormed into the building, I was hit by a blast of hot air. The ground was soft. My shoes slid in soft mud. I struggled to keep my balance as I roared forward.

It was darker than the night in here. I couldn't see a thing. A sharp aroma greeted me, heavy and sour. I heard soft cries, animal bleats.

My shoes pounded the soft goo. I heard a splash— and lurched forward. My hands shot up as I lost my balance. My sneakers slapped the mud but couldn't catch hold. I fell hard, fell face forward.

My body hit the soft, wet ground. My head burrowed into the mud. And I slid . . . slid . . . suddenly aware of the putrid odor . . . the foul odor of the air, of the mud, a powerful smell that made me choke and gag.

Stunned, I raised my head from the muck. Animal grunts and squeals surrounded me. I struggled to my feet. My clothes were covered in thick mud. The mud caked my face and my hair.

I had landed on my hands. They throbbed and ached as I rubbed the mud off them on the front of my overcoat.

A flickering light behind me made me spin around. I was gasping for air. But I inhaled the sick smell with each breath. My whole body shook. Where was I?

The orange-yellow light grew brighter as a man approached. He was big and broad and stern faced, carrying a flaming torch. He wore a gray flannel shirt under a huge pair of overalls. His bulging belly bounced with each step.

He didn't take his gaze off me as he stepped carefully through the mud and around the deep puddles. Finally, he stopped and held the torch high, studying me in its circle of light.

"What are you doing in my pigpen?" he demanded in a booming voice.

I gasped. "Pigpen?"

He looked me up and down. "You're covered in slops. You're going to smell for a year!"

Suddenly, in the light from the torch, I could see the enormous hogs lined up on both sides of me. About two dozen fat pigs all staring at me, honking and bleating.

The smell . . .

Yes. The smell. The thick muck stuck to my clothes, my face, my hair. I pulled a soft, rotted corncob from under my collar.

My stomach lurched. I was about to puke. I forced it down.

"The other kids . . . ," I choked out. "They told me to run in here and—"

He spun around. "Other kids? I didn't see any other kids out there."

"The three kids from school," I said. "They brought me here. They said—"

I didn't finish my sentence. I dodged the big farmer and ran to the pigpen door, my sneakers slapping up mud. I burst outside, shouting, "Hey! Where are you? Hey!"

No one there.

The frozen air hit me and made me gasp. The moon

had disappeared behind clouds. I squinted into the total darkness.

No one.

I knew what they had done. It didn't take long to figure it out.

The joke was on me. I was so desperate to escape, I had fallen for it.

Or rather, I had fallen *right into* it.

A pigpen. Not a time tunnel. A filthy smelly pigpen.

Had they taught me a lesson with their mean joke? I was too cold and mud-caked and putrid smelling to think about it.

Torchlight washed over me. I turned to find the farmer standing behind me. "You'd better go home, son," he said. "Where do you live?"

I shook my head sadly. "Nowhere," I said. "I don't live anywhere. Can I . . . Can I come in your house and take a bath?"

He squinted at me. "Afraid not. I can't let you in my house. You smell too bad. But you can sleep here in the pigpen tonight, if you like."

Suddenly, the pigs all started honking and bleating. As if they didn't want me, either.

17

Luckily, the farmer took pity on me and changed his mind. He let me sleep on a wood cot in his back room. I scrubbed myself at his pump in the kitchen. His wife was kind enough to lend me a nightshirt as she washed my clothes.

Lying on the hard cot, shivering under the thin blanket they had given me, I couldn't get to sleep. I peered out the tiny back window, up at the pale moon as it slid in and out of the clouds.

I knew why the Ghost of Christmas Past had brought me back to this awful place. To learn about the Golden Rule and all that junk about why it's better to be a nice boy.

But all I could think about was revenge.

I thought of scheme after scheme. But I decided none of them would work. It would be seriously impossible to get revenge on Prescott, Benjamin, and Emily-Ann. Because they lived here and knew everyone at school and knew the village. And I didn't know anything about anything. I didn't even have a place to live.

"But maybe I can at least get them in a little trouble at school," I told myself. I decided I'd tell Mr. Dulwich that the three of them kidnapped me and threw me into a pigpen because I'm the new kid. At least, he would give them a strong lecture about that.

The next morning, I thanked the farmer and his wife. I raced to school, my open coat flapping behind me, my sneakers crunching on the hardened snow.

The red morning sun reflected off the snow. The wind had stopped swirling. The bare trees stood perfectly still.

I was breathing hard as I reached the school building. The front hall was empty. I realized I was early. I stopped and caught my breath before going into Mr. Dulwich's classroom.

He was at the back of the room, leaning over a small Christmas tree. I saw that he was attaching slender white candles to the branches. His black suit jacket was unbuttoned. His pointy collar stuck up from his shirt. His eyeglasses glistened from the sunlight pouring in through the window.

He turned as I stepped into the room. "Mr. Dulwich—?" I started.

He cleared his throat. "Can I help you, young man?"

"I . . . I need to report three students," I said. I took a few steps closer. I hadn't expected to feel this tense. "They grabbed me last night and . . . and forced me to spend the night in a pigpen."

It was *almost* true. Maybe I made it sound a little worse than it was. Why should I tell him they had tricked me?

Mr. Dulwich set down a candle and pushed the glasses up on his nose. "Three students? From my class? Why did they do that to you?"

"They didn't like me, I guess," I replied. "They said they didn't like new kids."

He nodded. "Can you tell me their names?"

"Yes," I said. "Prescott, Benjamin, and Emily-Ann."

His eyebrows went up. "Please repeat those names, young man."

So I repeated them.

"I believe you've made a mistake," he said. "Perhaps you are in the wrong classroom?"

"No way," I replied. "I was here yesterday. They were here, too, and—"

Mr. Dulwich shook his head. "No. Not here. I am afraid I have no students named Prescott, Benjamin, or Emily-Ann."

18

"Of course you do," I insisted. "They sat near the front and—"

Mr. Dulwich took long strides to his desk. His heavy shoes made the floorboards squeak. He shoved aside some papers on his desk and raised a black notebook.

I stepped up to the desk. "Is that your class list?"

He nodded and shoved the open book toward me. "This is my attendance book. You can see with your own eyes," he said. "There are no students in my class named Prescott, Benjamin, or Emily-Ann."

I let my eyes run down the list. He was telling the truth.

I suddenly had a heavy feeling in the pit of my stomach. I had to force myself to breathe.

What is going down here?

Mr. Dulwich said something, but my thoughts were too loud. I couldn't hear him. He squeezed the sleeve of my overcoat. "Young man, I asked you a question. What is *your* name?"

"Rick. Rick Scroogeman," I said. "Remember? I'm the new kid. I arrived yesterday?"

He took the attendance book from my hand, and his finger rolled down the list of his students. He took his time, reading carefully.

Finally. He raised his eyes to me. "I'm afraid you aren't in my class, either, Mr. Scroogeman."

"But—but—but—" I sputtered like a motorboat. The heavy feeling in my stomach spread to my whole body.

"You should check Mr. Harrison's class," he said, closing the book. "Perhaps since you are new—"

"No," I said. "I'm not in another class. I'm in *your* class."

He shrugged. "Sorry. You're not here."

"Then *where am I?*" I cried.

"Nowhere," he said softly.

And as he said that word, he faded away.

Nowhere.

The word lingered in my mind. And repeated. *Nowhere. Nowhere. Nowhere.*

Mr. Dulwich vanished slowly, and the classroom faded with him. His desk shimmered and then was gone. The color seeped from the walls until I was surrounded by gray. Solid gray everywhere I turned. The little Christmas tree was the last thing I saw.

And then there I stood, like I was suspended in space, in a solid, silent world of gray . . . no shades . . . all the same gray . . . until I didn't know if I was seeing or not. Didn't know if my eyes were open or closed.

Then, when someone grabbed my shoulder, I opened my mouth and screamed.

I spun around. And cut off my scream as I saw a short, pudgy man in a black-and-white-checkered suit beside me. He had a funny face. I mean, the kind of face that makes you laugh. A big pink lightbulb of a nose and round black owl eyes, and a tiny red mouth shaped like a heart.

He had ringlets of curly orange hair falling from beneath a tall, shiny black top hat. He wore a red bow tie and had a matching red flower in the lapel of his checkered jacket. The flower looked like the kind that squirts water.

"Are you ready to come with me, Scroogeman?" he said. He had a high voice and kind of sang the words instead of speaking them.

"Who are you supposed to be?" I demanded.

His round cheeks turned red. So did his bulby nose. "I am the Ghost of Christmas Present," he said in his odd singsong.

For a moment, he disappeared into the gray. Then he came back in full color.

"You're the Ghost of Christmas Presents?" I said. "Did you bring me my Christmas presents?"

He flickered again and nearly disappeared.

"I am the Ghost of Christmas *Present*," he said. "I shall take you to your family—if you have learned the lessons of the past."

My heart skipped a beat. "You'll take me to my family? Really?" I cried happily. "Oh yes. I learned a lot. I learned a lot of lessons from the past."

Okay, I was lying. You know it, and I know it. But *he* didn't have to know it—did he?

He stared hard at me, so hard his big bulby nose twitched. "And what lessons have you learned, Scroogeman?"

"Well . . ."

Think fast. Think fast.

"I learned to be a good guy and always be nice to people and to think about other people's feelings, not just my own."

The ghost crossed his arms in front of him. "I thought you were a better liar than that," he said.

"Oh, I am. I am," I replied. "Just give me a chance."

"What did you *really* learn?" the ghost asked.

"Not to go running into a pigpen at night?"

He gripped my shoulder again. His grip wasn't gentle. He tightened his fingers until I flinched. "Ow."

"I'm taking you to your family, Scroogeman," he said. "You have much to learn in the present day."

"I . . . I get to go back to Mom and Charlie?" I asked.

He didn't reply. He stared straight forward. We started to drop.

I gasped. We were falling fast, falling straight down through the solid gray. The cold air came up to meet us. It was like falling through clouds.

That was a dream I had a lot. Just falling straight down through clouds. Falling . . . falling . . . and never landing.

The ghost's top hat flew off his head. His hand dug into my shoulder. We plunged down, then started to slow. Colors swirled up in the gray, bright flashes of green and blue and red. So bright, I shut my eyes.

When I opened them, I was standing on something solid. A floor in a living room. My eyes took a long time to focus. I saw a green carpet, stained and torn. The walls were covered in a green wallpaper. Some of it was curling off at the top.

Blinking hard, I saw a scrawny Christmas tree behind a low black couch. It had an angel tilted at the top and only a few tree decorations hanging on its skinny branches. A single flame flickered in the fireplace. A MERRY CHRISTMAS banner hung crookedly over the mantel.

The Ghost of Christmas Present was pushing down his wiry orange hair with both hands. Without his top hat, his hair had blown in all directions during our fall.

I tapped him on one arm. "Whoa. You got it wrong," I said. "This isn't my house. You've made a big mistake."

"Ghosts don't make mistakes," he replied. "I've never heard of a ghost making a mistake."

"Marley's ghost made a mistake," I said. "He tried to haunt the wrong house."

"Who is Marley?" the ghost asked. "Am I supposed to know him?"

"Forget about him," I said. "I don't live here. Look at this place. It's a dump."

He pursed his tiny, heart-shaped lips. "This is your home now, Scroogeman. It's very different from *your* home. I'm hoping it will make you appreciate your *old* life."

"I do!" I protested. "I *do* appreciate my old life. Take me to my house. I'll appreciate it. I swear!"

"My hope is that your new family will show you how you are mistaken about Christmas," the ghost said, fiddling with his red bow tie. "I think they can show you the true meaning of the holiday."

I tugged at his sleeve. "And if I learn it, can I go back to my family?"

He narrowed his eyes at me. "You have a lot to learn before you can ever think of going back."

Those words sent a chill to the back of my neck.

The ghost turned away from me. He motioned toward the small dining room. "This is your family now, Scroogeman."

I saw a ragged-looking man and woman and a pale, scrawny girl, who was about eight or nine. They were standing awkwardly at the dining room table.

The woman had scraggly brown hair falling down the sides of her narrow, lined face. Her eyes were red, as if she'd been crying. She wore a long brown house-dress under a square white apron. The apron was dotted with brown and yellow stains.

The man was thin and tired looking, too. His back

was a little bent. He leaned on a wooden cane. His streaky gray hair was pulled behind his head in a stub of a ponytail. He wore a black sweatshirt over baggy maroon sweatpants.

The girl was kind of cute. She had wavy brown-blond hair and big blue eyes. She wore a blue smiley-face T-shirt pulled down over faded denim jeans, torn at both knees. She kept motioning impatiently to me. She wanted me to come over to them.

But I turned to the ghost. "Please—take me out of here. It's Christmas Eve. Take me to my real family. Please."

"Merry Christmas, Scroogeman," he said. Then he vanished.

I felt a *pop* of cold air. And he was gone.

"Come to the table, Scroogeman," the woman said. "You're late. You know it's time for Christmas Eve dinner."

"Come sit down, sonny boy," the man said. "If you stand there any longer, I'll swat you. I swear I will."

Sonny boy?

They acted as if they knew me, as if I really belonged in their family.

I was suddenly starving. My stomach grumbled. I couldn't remember the last time I had a meal.

I crossed the shabby living room to the dining room. "Okay. I'll play along," I said. "What's for dinner?"

The woman gave me a thin smile. "We are each going to have a juicy ripe plum."

Was there something wrong with my hearing?

Did she just say we were going to have a plum for Christmas dinner?

I let out a sigh and walked over to them. "Where should I sit?" I asked.

"Scroogeman, stop acting the clown," the mother said. "You know where you sit. Why are you acting so strange tonight? Because it's Christmas Eve?"

I took a chance and sat down next to the girl. Her name was Ashley. I figured it out because that's what her parents kept calling her. She kept poking me with one finger and tickling my ribs when the parents weren't looking. Just like a little sister.

Didn't she know I don't belong here?

The table was nearly bare. The four dinner plates didn't match. On each plate, I saw a purple plum.

"Are we having turkey or ham after the plum?" I asked.

My new father scowled at me. "Scroogeman, we are having a plum for dinner, and let's be grateful for that."

My stomach rumbled again. "That's all? A plum?" I cried. My voice cracked.

"Slice it very thin, and it will go a long way," my new mom said. "Show him, Ashley."

Ashley picked up her knife and began cutting her plum into very thin slices. "This looks so juicy," she said. "I love Christmas Eve dinner."

"We always have a turkey *and* a ham," I said. "And a big layer cake for dessert."

"In your dreams?" the dad said. He pushed a slice of plum into his mouth and chewed it as if it were a chunk of steak. "Is that what you dream about, Scroogeman?"

The mom sighed. "A tall layer cake. Yes, that's something to dream about. Maybe someday . . ." Her voice trailed off.

I sliced my plum the way Ashley did. I took a bite.

Mine wasn't quite ripe. But I didn't care. I was so hungry, I planned to eat the pit.

I finished my plum in about ten seconds. When Ashley turned away, I grabbed three or four slices off her plate, and I ate those, too.

"Hey!" she shouted angrily. "Mom—Scroogeman ate some of my plum."

"It's Christmas, dear," the mom scolded. "Be generous." Mom turned to me. "What else do you dream about?"

"I dream about my Christmas presents," I said.

"Well, I have a nice present for the two of you," the dad said. "It isn't anything special. You know how hard it has been for me at the factory. Especially with my bad back."

He climbed to his feet and crossed the room. He picked up two small items from the top of a cabinet. He handed one to Ashley and one to me. A smile spread over his face. "These were made with love," he said. "Made with my own two hands."

I gazed at mine. It was a tiny piece of molded plastic, very smooth, shaped like an old-fashioned whistle, painted blue with smile emojis up and down it. Ashley's was just like mine, only painted green.

I raised my eyes to Dad, who was still smiling. "What are they?" I asked.

"Key chains," he said. "They let me use the three-D printer at the factory, and I made them. My own design."

"Love it!" Ashley cried. She jumped up and hugged her dad.

"Yeah. Awesome," I said. "Thanks. Awesome present." I tucked it into my jeans pocket.

"Maybe someday you'll have keys to put on them," the mom said.

I slipped the last plum slice off Ashley's plate and swallowed it before she could try to grab it back. "And that's it for presents?" I said, thinking of the big stack of gifts in the closet back home.

"Christmas is a time of giving," Mom said, flashing me a sad smile. "We've always taught you that, Scroogeman."

"But you're not giving us anything else?" I said.

"We gave some of your clothes and some of your old games and books away," Ashley said. "We gave them away to—"

"You *what*?" I cried.

"To those less fortunate than us," she finished her sentence.

I stared at her. My mouth hung open. Was that the lesson I was supposed to learn about Christmas? To give my stuff away? They had to be joking.

We just had a plum for dinner. And we got plastic key chains for gifts? And they were talking about people *less fortunate*? Are you kidding me?

"Are you ready for our Christmas Eve dessert?" Mom asked. She disappeared into the kitchen. She returned a few seconds later carrying a plate of green grapes.

"My favorite!" Ashley cried, clapping her hands.

What a weirdo.

Mom dropped four grapes on each plate. "Enjoy," she said.

Dad took his knife and sliced each grape into two halves. Then he ate the halves slowly, holding them up one by one, chewing each one a long time. "Now let's do our annual Christmas tradition," he said. "Let's go around the table and tell what we are grateful for."

Excuse me? Was I supposed to be grateful for a plum and four grapes?

Dad started to talk about what he was thankful for. It had something to do with his back being better. I didn't listen. I was staring at something hanging on the kitchen wall. Squinting into the kitchen, I saw the calendar stuck on the side of a cabinet.

And when I saw the year, I had to force myself not to utter a cry. Not to pump my fists in the air and leap onto the table and do a celebration dance.

It was *this year*. The ghost hadn't lied. I really *was* in the *present*.

I was back in the right year. Back where I belonged.

And as my new mom yammered on about something she was happy about, I instantly realized what I was happy about. I was happy that I could escape from this house and go home.

No problem.

I just wait till they're asleep. I run out of this tacky falling-apart house. I find someone who will lend me a phone. I call my real mom and she comes and gets me.

How easy is that?

It wouldn't take long before I was home with Mom and Charlie, in time to celebrate my birthday and Christmas, and eat till I burst, and enjoy all my presents (and Charlie's, too).

Ashley poked me in the ribs, jarring me from my happy thoughts. "Go ahead, Scroogeman. We're waiting for you."

I gazed around the table. "What?"

"We're waiting," she said. "What are you thankful for?"

"Well . . ." I thought hard.

What was the right answer?

"I'm just thankful to be able to enjoy Christmas Eve dinner with my wonderful family," I said.

That brought smiles to all of their faces. Score one for Rick Scroogeman.

"Scroogeman is right," Ashley said. "People have to care about each other. Whether they're rich or as poor as our family. People have to love each other and stick together."

"Yes. Stick together," I said. "I'm all about that, Ashley. For sure. I'm all over that, you know. Sticking together is totally my thing."

Of course, I was thinking of only one thing—escape.

I'm thankful to be getting out of this dump, and I'm thankful never to have a plum and a few grapes for dinner again. Good-bye and good luck.

Ashley helped her parents clear the dinner table. There wasn't much to clear. I mean, there hadn't been any food on the table.

I stood up and stretched. I wondered how early my new mom and dad go to bed. I planned to escape this place as soon as they were asleep.

"Let's go, Scroogeman. Come on. Before it gets dark." Ashley tugged my hand. "Get your coat."

"Huh? Where are we going?" I asked.

She jerked my arm. "Don't act dumb. You know where we're going. To build our Christmas Eve snowmen." She pulled on a ragged gray hoodie and dragged me to the front door.

I guessed that building snowmen was another family tradition I didn't know about. I pulled on a coat I found in the front closet and followed Ashley outside.

It was a cold, windy evening. A red sun was lowering behind the trees. I saw a row of tiny houses, all very close together, lined up across the street behind small, square front yards. This was definitely a poor neighborhood. But all the houses had Christmas lights and decorations in their front windows.

I shivered. The snow in the front yard was at least a foot deep and very crusty. Good for packing.

I couldn't resist. I grabbed up a big handful of snow and molded it into a snowball. Then I cried out, "Think fast!" and smashed it into Ashley's face. I held it there, rubbing it over her cheeks and eyes.

Ha-ha. She sputtered and spit and started to choke. It was a riot. She was totally surprised.

I backed up quickly. I knew she'd try to pay me back.

But no. She wiped the icy snow off her face, then pulled her hoodie tighter over her hair. "Don't mess around, Scroogeman," she snapped. "It's going to be dark soon."

She pointed to a spot near the curb. "You build one and I'll build one," she said. "We need two of them to be on guard."

I stared at her. "On guard? On guard for *what?*" I asked.

She narrowed her eyes. She lowered her voice to a whisper. "You'll see," she said.

My snowman was bigger than Ashley's. And smoother and more round. We built them facing each other at the bottom of the yard.

We both used chunks of coal for their eyes. I used my finger to dig a big, angry scowl on my snowman's face. Ashley placed an orange-and-black wool cap on her snowman's head.

It was kind of fun. A little babyish, maybe. And I kept thinking about how I was going to run away and call my mom and never see this neighborhood again.

"What city is this?" I asked Ashley as we headed back to the house. "Where are we exactly?"

She gave me a shove. "Don't ask stupid questions."

"No. Really," I said.

But she tossed her hoodie into the closet and disappeared into her room.

Mom greeted me in the living room. "I'm sorry this wasn't a great Christmas Eve, Scroogeman," she said. I thought I saw tears in her eyes. "Ashley was right. The only good thing about the holiday this year is that we're all here together."

Not for long, I thought.

I said good night and made my way down the short back hall to my room. I dropped down on my bed. "Ouch!" I should have looked first. There was no mattress on the bed. The sheet and blanket were spread over a hard board.

How could anyone sleep on a board?

Something brushed my ankle. I heard a scraping sound under the bed.

Oh, wow. There were mice in the room! Was I really expected to sleep on a hard board with mice scampering around me all night?

The Ghost of Christmas Present said this family could teach me a lot. But I sure wasn't learning anything I wanted to learn. Was I missing the point? Was I supposed to be learning something about the meaning of Christmas?

I don't think so.

I sat there on the edge of the hard bed, tapping my foot on the floor. Waiting. Just waiting.

I thought about Mom and Charlie back in my real home. I knew they must be terribly worried about me. Mom must be out of her mind. They were having the worst Christmas ever.

But not for long. "I'm coming home," I murmured to myself. "I'll be home soon."

I waited until I heard my new dad turn off all the lights. The house was completely dark now. I heard the creaking floorboards as he and my new mom went into their bedroom.

Then I waited some more . . . waited for them to fall asleep.

The house was silent now. Gusts of wind rattled my bedroom window. I could see a pale sliver of a moon low in the sky.

Something brushed past my ankle. I kicked at it. Missed. Heard it squeak and scuttle away.

I stood up and stretched. Then I crept out of my room on tiptoe, trying to step lightly so the bare wooden floors wouldn't creak.

I moved quickly through the darkness. I kept peering back, afraid someone might be following me. But no. The others were in their rooms. I grabbed my coat from the closet, carefully, silently slid open the front door, and stepped outside.

"You lose, Ghost of Christmas Present," I muttered out loud. "I'm outta here, you clown."

I zipped my jacket. Lowered my head against the swirling wind. Tucked my hands in the pockets. Then I began to walk quickly over the hard, crunchy snow toward the street.

I'd gone about four steps when someone slid in front of me. Someone big, blocking my way.

No. Wait. Not someone. Not a human.

I stopped. And under the pale yellow moonlight, I stared at the big creature. Stared into the scowling face of my snowman.

22

I uttered a startled gasp. Then I dodged to the right.

To my shock, the snowman slid over the snow and blocked me again.

I lowered my head and tried to swerve around it. But it moved quickly, silently gliding over the snow, staying close, pushing its big bulk in front of me.

And as I gaped in horror at the moving snowman, its coal eyes lit up. The eyes appeared to flame, first yellow-orange and then an angry blazing red.

"Nooooo!" A howl escaped my throat. This was *impossible*!

I couldn't take my eyes off the glowing coals. I forced myself to look away. Spun to the right. Maybe

I could escape through the backyard instead of the front.

I stumbled forward. My boots slid on the crusty surface—and I toppled right into *the other snowman*. Ashley's snowman with the orange-and-black wool cap on its head. Its eyes were glowing red, too.

I'm living in a horror movie. My first thought.

They had me trapped here, one big snowman bumping up against my front, the other behind me, sliding from side to side, waiting for me to make a move.

Suddenly, my fear was replaced by anger. I felt all my muscles tighten.

Why were these big snow creatures trying to keep me from returning to my family?

I opened my mouth in a furious scream. And screeched at both of them: "Get back! Get back or I'll destroy you. I'll knock your heads off. Get *away* from me!"

They didn't move. Remained in place, blocking my escape.

I could feel the rage swell in my chest. "Get *away!*" I screamed again. I pulled my arm back and shot my fist as hard as I could into my snowman's frozen head.

I expected the head to topple off the body. But it didn't budge. The punch didn't even make the snowman slide back an inch.

Breathing hard, I tried to pull my arm away. But my fist was stuck . . . stuck in the snowman's tightly packed face.

"Nooooo!" I uttered a howl and pulled again. Jerked my whole body around, trying to twist myself free. But my hand was stuck tight in the icy head.

"Let me go! Let me go!" I was screaming wildly. I raised my other fist and slammed it into the snowman's body.

Again, the snowman didn't seem to feel it. I tugged myself back—but now *both hands* were stuck in its icy grip. I pulled and pulled again, leaning as far back as I could, but I couldn't free them.

And now I felt the cold begin to seep up my arms. It was like I was becoming as cold as the snowman. I was gasping for breath, my heart pounding so hard in my chest, it hurt.

I cried out as I felt the other snowman bump up behind me. It bumped me hard and pressed itself against my back.

Like an ice cream sandwich, I thought. A crazy thought.

The cold tightened my arms, crept over my chest, began to sweep over my whole body.

I'm freezing here, I thought. *My brain . . . my brain is freezing, too. So hard to . . . to breathe. I'm going to freeze to death out here.*

With a hard shudder, I shut my eyes as the two icy mountains of snow pressed in on me. Tighter . . . tighter . . .

23

And then the cold seeped away. I opened my eyes. The snowman in front of me was changing. The big round head began to sag.

Was it melting?

No. The big snow creature took a step back. It appeared to quake and quiver, vibrating noisily. The smooth white snow suddenly had black spots. And as I stared in surprise, the black spots became a checkered suit. Checkered jacket and pants.

The snowman face melted away, revealing a round pink nose, dark eyes, a heart-shaped mouth underneath. Curly orange hair sprouted on its head.

My mouth hung open. I couldn't breathe. I was staring at the Ghost of Christmas Present.

Behind me, the other snowman stood stiffly in place, its coal eyes alert, as if watching for trouble.

The ghost brushed the last clumps of snow off the front of his suit with both hands, then straightened the flower in his lapel. He gazed at me coldly and shook his head. "I'm disappointed in you, Scroogeman."

"I—I—I—" I stood there sputtering. I was speechless. I think my brain was still frozen.

"Ashley told you these snowmen were guards," the ghost said. "Guards to keep you from escaping. Did you think she was joking?"

"No," I said. "I just wanted—"

"You wanted to go home. I know," the ghost said. "But you were supposed to learn something about love and caring from this family. You were supposed to learn about what's important at holiday time." He sighed. "Instead, you try to run away."

"I . . . I think I'll learn those things better with my real family," I said. "I miss them a lot." I wasn't lying to him. I really meant it.

"I'm going to take you back to your neighborhood, Scroogeman," the ghost said, brushing powdery snow off one shoulder.

"Back to my neighborhood? So I can go home?" I cried.

He shook his head. "You're not ready to go home. I'm taking you to your neighborhood for another lesson. Perhaps this time you will catch on and realize what your bad attitude has cost you."

"Where?" I demanded. "Where are you taking me?"

"To a party," he said. "Your friend Lucy Copperfield is having a Christmas Eve party."

"I love to party," I said. "I'm a party animal. Ask anyone."

"I don't think you will love this party, Scroogeman. I think you will find some unhappy surprises tonight."

Then, without warning, I felt myself lifted off the ground. I gasped and raised both arms as I flew over the shabby little house, over the treetops. I saw the snowman tilt his head up, his coal eyes following me as I soared higher.

The Ghost of Christmas Present flew beside me. The jacket of his checkered suit flapped at his sides like wings. His red hair flew above his head like a pennant.

The wind rushed at us, so powerful and cold, I couldn't breathe. We sailed into heavy clouds. I could no longer see the houses below or the trees or the ground. I was surrounded by swirling, roaring gray, pounded by wind gusts that froze my face.

I shut my eyes and listened to the whistle and roar of our flight.

When I opened them, I was floating low over a snow-covered block of houses. The ghost flew beside me as we slowed and dropped lower. Suddenly, I recognized the house below us. Lucy Copperfield's house.

My heart started to pound. Lucy's house was only a block away from mine. I raised my arms again and tried to push myself forward. I wanted to keep flying, to see my house, to see Mom and Charlie.

But the ghost and I landed on our feet in front of Lucy's house. The windows were all lighted. A Christmas wreath hung on the front door. Santa and Rudolph the Reindeer decorations filled the living-room window.

"Please . . . let me go home." The words came out in a choked whisper.

The Ghost of Christmas Present didn't reply. He gave me a gentle push—and we floated through the front wall of the house.

Blinking in the bright light, I was standing in

Lucy's living room. I still felt the cold of the wind on my cheeks. I brushed down my hair with both hands.

My heavy overcoat had disappeared. Now I found myself wearing a red hoodie over faded denim jeans. When my eyes could finally focus, I saw a tall Christmas tree. Brightly wrapped presents with red and green ribbons were piled under the tree. A fire danced in a wide fireplace under a mantelpiece with red candles on either end.

I turned from the fireplace and the tree and saw my friends. Lucy Copperfield was handing a red tree ornament to Davey Pittman. They both wore red-and-green Christmas sweaters. Lucy had a silver ribbon tied in her hair. Davey turned to hang the decoration on a branch of the pine tree.

My heart was pounding like a bass drum now. I was so happy to be back, to see my good friends again.

"Hey, guys! I'm back!" I shouted. I ran up to them. "I'm back! Hey, I'm back!"

They didn't turn or look at me. Lucy took a glass Santa ornament and, standing on tiptoe, dangled it onto a tall branch.

"Hey, guys!" I tried again. "Hi! You won't believe where I've been! But I'm back just in time for your party!"

The Ghost of Christmas Present strode up beside me. "They can't hear you, Scroogeman," he said.

I uttered a shocked cry. "Huh?"

"They can't see or hear you," he said. "I didn't bring you here to join the party."

"But—but—these are my friends," I sputtered. "I know they've *got* to miss me. Why can't I be at the party?"

The ghost narrowed his eyes at me. "Are they really your friends? Did Lucy invite you to her party?"

I thought about it. "Well . . . no. She probably forgot. But . . . everyone knows that I'm the *best* at parties. How can you have a party without Rick Scroogeman? *No way.*"

The doorbell rang. Lucy hurried to answer the door.

"You're here to watch them, Scroogeman," the ghost said. "You're here to watch and observe. And perhaps learn the truth about yourself."

He vanished in a puff of cold air.

"Hey, Davey!" I shouted. "*You* can see me—can't you? Davey? How's it going? Huh? What's up?"

Davey Pittman lifted a shiny silver Christmas bell from the decorations box and stood trying to decide on a good place for it on the tree.

Shaking my head, I trotted past him and followed

Lucy to the front door. She was greeting Josh Cratchit. "Hey, J-J-J-osh!" I called.

He stamped snow off his shoes and handed Lucy a wrapped present. I realized he didn't hear me. He took a few steps toward the living room, then stopped and peered around.

He waved at Davey. Then he turned to Lucy. "Who-who is coming to the p-p-party?"

"Just Billy O'Brian and a few other kids from our class," she told him.

"Not Scroogeman?" he asked.

"Scroogeman? Of course not!" Lucy replied. She made a disgusted face. "Why would I invite Scroogeman?"

Huh?

Why did Lucy say that? We've been friends forever.

Josh shrugged out of his coat and hung it on the coat hook behind the door. "G-good. I was worried."

I stared at him with my mouth open. This didn't make any sense. "Hey, Josh—I thought we were good pals," I said.

"Scroogeman ruins every party," Davey said, hanging a red ball on the tree. "He takes over the party and ruins it for everyone else."

"He's a total jerk," Lucy said. "And the sad thing is, he doesn't even know it. He doesn't have a clue."

Hey, whoa.

What's up with my friends? Were they bad-mouthing me because they knew I was standing there?

"Guys! Guys! Give me a break," I said. I walked over to Davey Pittman and gave him a hard punch on the shoulder.

Oh, wow. My hand went right through him. He didn't feel a thing.

I pressed my face against his cheek and screamed at the top of my lungs into his ear. "CAN YOU HEAR ME, DAVEY?"

He didn't flinch or pull away. He handed a tree ornament to Josh. "Lucy's family always decorates their tree on Christmas Eve," Davey told him. "It's their family tradition."

I waved my hands in front of Lucy's face. She didn't blink.

I tried to mess up her perfect hair. But I could see through my hand. And I couldn't feel her hair at all.

I took a step back. I couldn't help it. I felt stunned. I mean, I should be the life of the party, right? Here I was, ready to have fun with everyone. But . . . it was like I wasn't there.

Billy O'Brian showed up next, then some other kids from school. I watched them grab cups of Christmas punch and cookies. My stomach rumbled. All I'd had to eat was a plum and a few grapes.

I reached for a stack of Christmas cookies but my hand couldn't pick them up.

Oh, wow, I thought, *this is so unfair.*

In front of the fireplace, Sheena Pryce, a girl I was never friends with, was saying something about me. I didn't hear what she said, but the two boys she was talking to burst out laughing.

"Lucy, this is an awesome party—especially since Scroogeman isn't here," Billy O'Brian said.

"Hey, Belly—you're hurting my feelings!" I shouted. I grabbed his nose and twisted it. Only my hand went right through his head. He didn't feel a thing.

I swallowed hard. I suddenly realized my feelings *were* hurt. I felt totally sad, like a heavy wave of sadness had rolled down over me.

"I thought you guys were my friends." My voice came out shaky and high.

Lucy said something else about me, and they all laughed.

They don't like me. It's true. They really don't like me.

"S-S-Scroogeman makes me f-feel so bad," Josh

said, shaking his head. "I h-h-hate my stutter. I'm t-trying so hard to get rid of it. B-but Scroogeman makes fun of it every t-t-time he sees me. And Miss D-D-Dorrit lets him get away with it."

The poor guy had tears in his eyes. Because of me? I didn't want to hurt him. I was just having fun with him.

"I'm sorry, Josh," I shouted. "I didn't know it made you feel so bad. I guess I just wasn't thinking. I promise I'll never do it again."

He didn't hear me.

I gazed around. "Ghost, where are you? I want to apologize to Josh, but he can't hear me."

No sign of the ghost.

Billy O'Brian poured himself another cup of punch. "The Christmas play was going to be so much fun," he said. "I couldn't wait to play Santa. But now we have no costumes, and Mr. Pickwick had to cancel the play."

"It's like Sick Rick ruined Christmas for everyone," Lucy said.

Sick Rick? Did Lucy call me that, too?

I had a heavy feeling in the pit of my stomach. My friends *hated* me. They all started telling stories about what a bad dude I am. Even kids I didn't know very well had bad things to say about me.

I backed into a corner and dropped cross-legged onto the floor. I felt kind of dizzy. I guess I was in shock. It was like I was struck by lightning or something.

I didn't know how to deal with this, the idea that everyone hated me so much. All the fun things I did with them—the dance lessons, my water fountain joke, messing up Lucy's perfect hair . . . I thought it was all funny.

And now, sitting there invisible, listening to them complain about me, calling me Sick Rick and even worse names, I suddenly *did* feel sick.

"I don't have any friends," I told myself. "No friends at all. No one likes me." I had to say the words to believe it, I guess.

I'd never cried in my life. Crying is for babies. That's what I always believed. Whenever I saw someone cry, it always made me laugh.

But now my chin was quivering. My whole face was trembling. I could feel teardrops cover my eyes.

No! I wiped them away. I crossed my arms in front of my chest and watched the party. They held an Ugly Christmas Sweater Contest. Davey won with his awful Rudolph the Reindeer sweater. On one side of the sweater, Rudolph's nose actually lit up and blinked on and off.

They had pizza and hot dogs. They sang a few Christmas carols.

"Lucy, open my present," Davey insisted.

It was a big box. Everyone gathered around to watch Lucy tear off the wrapping and open it. She pulled out a big balloonlike thing. No. It was a punching bag. An inflated punching bag. You know. You punch it and it bops right back up.

Lucy held it up, a look of surprise on her face. "Davey? You bought me a punching bag?"

"Look at its face," Davey said. "Don't you see why I bought it? It looks a lot like Scroogeman!"

I jumped to my feet and walked closer. Well . . . it had my dark hair, and the face was a little like mine.

"Go ahead. Punch Scroogeman out," Billy O'Brian shouted.

Lucy gave the thing a hard punch. It tilted back almost to the floor, then bounced up. She punched it again. Harder. "Take that, Scroogeman!"

"I want a t-t-turn," Josh Cratchit said. He started punching the bag across the room.

As I watched in shock, other kids eagerly took their turns punching, punching me. Bopping the bag harder and harder. And laughing. All of them laughing as they hit me.

Believe me, I felt every punch. I felt them in the pit of my stomach.

Punch. Punch. Punch.

I was doubled over in pain. I didn't really feel their punches. I felt their anger and their hatred.

Punch. Punchpunchpunch.

The room filled with shouts and laughter. They were having so much fun punching Scroogeman. "Best present ever!" Lucy shouted over all the voices.

"But I can change!" I cried. "I can change. Really!"

I knew they couldn't hear me. But I shouted anyway. "I can change! I can be a good friend! Do you hear me? Please—hear me. I can change!"

Someone punched the bag so hard, it flew into the air and crashed into the Christmas tree. Ornaments went flying. Everyone suddenly hushed.

I took a step back. I remembered where I was. One block from my house. I could get away from this horrible party. I could run home and see Mom and Charlie, people who loved me . . . People who didn't hate me.

I turned and took two steps to the front door. And stopped.

Whoa. Where *was* everybody?

They'd disappeared. The room stood empty. No kids. No one.

And then the room vanished, too. I was surrounded by nothing. Pale blue nothing. What was I standing on? The sky?

I spun around. I gazed up, then down. The room was gone. The whole house was gone. If I was floating in the sky, there were no clouds, no sun or moon, just this solid pale blue all around me.

I raised both hands and tried to fly. But no way. I felt as if I were hanging there, like a puppet, suspended by an invisible string.

A burst of cold air, and a silvery figure floated up beside me. A robot. A metal robot. "Who are you?" I cried.

The robot hummed to life. "I am the Ghost of Christmas Future," it announced in a tinny voice.

"Another ghost?" I said. "Can't I just go home? I think I've learned my lesson. Seriously."

"Come with me," the robot said in the tinny, metallic voice. "You have more to learn, Scroogeman. You have only begun to learn the truth about yourself."

"But my house is only a block away," I protested. "Please—let me go home. I learned a real lesson at that party. I know what I have to do now. I have to become a better friend."

"I am not convinced," it droned. Its metal hand closed over my hand. It felt cold and hard. "You need to see your future, Scroogeman. Then perhaps you will mean what you say."

We began to move, soaring higher into the solid blue.

"Wait. Stop! Where are you taking me?" I cried.

"To your future, as I said," it shouted, and we soared higher. "To the place you deserve. Where you will spend your days . . . forever."

That didn't sound good.

"Can we talk about this?" I asked.

"Another school?" I cried. "You're dropping me at another school?"

I stared at the tall black building. It looked like Dracula's castle, with two tall round towers on the sides. We were on a dirt path that led to the school. The robot ghost and I stood beside a wide flower bed. The flowers were all *black*.

"I'm not going to stay here," I said. I crossed my arms in front of me, trying to look tough. "That first ghost took me to a weird school where the kids were all mean to me. I've been there, done that."

The ghost locked its glassy eyes on me. "The other two ghosts tried to help you," it said, pronouncing each word like a computer. "You ruined Christmas for your friends and for your family. The ghosts tried to help you learn how to treat others and what Christmas should mean to you."

"I've learned a lot!" I cried. "I can change. Really. I've learned what I have to do."

"Scroogeman, you learned nothing," the ghost said. "Zero. Zip. Nada. Goose eggs. Nil. Nix. Naught. Zilch. Diddly squat."

I squinted at it. "Diddly squat?"

It nodded. "We robots say that a lot in the future."

I gazed at the tall towers of the huge school building. Were those *vultures* circling the towers?

"So you're dropping me at another school to help me learn—*what* exactly?" I said.

"I'm not here to help you, Scroogeman. I give up. Your school principal gave up on you, too. I'm not going to help you. I'm going to leave you here because this is where you belong. This is your future."

"But you're not giving me a chance," I said, my voice trembling. "Lucy's party changed me. I saw what my friends think of me and . . . and . . ."

I gazed up at the circling vultures, and a shiver rolled down my back. The black flowers in the big flower bed shivered, too, blown by a sudden cold wind.

The ghost ignored my pleas. The robot led me up

the dirt path toward the school entrance. The double doors in the front were black, the same shade as the whole building. "What is the name of this school?" I asked.

"It's called Dead Middle School," it replied.

I saw black skulls in a row on a window ledge. I could hear the flap of the vultures' wings overhead. The wind blew at my back, as if pushing me into this school.

"Dead Middle School?" I said. "What kind of name is that?"

"You'll find this school interesting, Scroogeman. They have a very good afterlife program."

I didn't understand. I just knew I didn't belong here. I turned to the robot ghost. "Take me home. Please," I begged. "I'll change. I'll be totally different."

It vanished in a puff of cold air.

The black double doors creaked open slowly. I stepped up to the entrance. "Dead Middle School," I murmured softly to myself. "Catchy name."

I took a deep breath and walked inside.

I blinked. I'd expected a dark dungeon. Black halls with cobwebbed ceilings and skulls over every door. I mean, the outside of the school looked like a castle from a horror movie. But the inside looked like a normal school.

I gazed down the brightly lit hall. The walls were yellow tile. Two rows of green metal lockers on either side. The classroom doors were bright colors and stood open. But I didn't hear any voices in the rooms.

My shoes clattered on the tile floor. I stopped in front of a glass trophy case. Inside, the shelves were filled with gleaming sports trophies. One trophy read: NATIONAL DEAD TENNIS CHAMPIONS, 2095.

2095? Huh?

A red-and-black banner was draped across the hall. It had a football painted on one side, and it read: CRUSH THEM, CADAVERS!

"What kind of animal is a cadaver?" I asked myself. I'd never heard that word.

I decided I had to find the main office and tell the principal that I'm here. Were they expecting me?

I strode quickly down the hall. Before I could find the office, a buzzer rang out. Kids came pouring out of the classrooms.

I stopped and stared. They looked like normal kids. The guys were in jeans and T-shirts. A lot of the girls wore short skirts with black tights underneath.

"The future looks a lot like my time," I told myself. "I think I could like this school."

I felt kind of excited. I wondered if I could make some new friends here. Maybe I could practice being nicer. Show everyone I could be a good dude.

Perhaps it wasn't so bad that the three Christmas ghosts had given up on me. Maybe I could have fun here before it was time to go back home.

But then I noticed something strange. No noise. No voices. The kids had just been let out of their classrooms, but they were all silent.

Must be a school rule, I thought. *No talking in the halls.*

"We'll have to change that," I muttered. The quiet was giving me the creeps.

"Yo, everyone," I shouted. "What's up?"

Kids stopped walking and turned to me. Their eyes were wide and blank. Their expressions were surprised. I guess no one broke the rule before.

Three or four kids walked up to me. They appeared to be about my age. They still hadn't made a sound.

A girl with pale green eyes studied me. She was very pretty. She wore a short pleated plaid skirt and a red top. Her light brown hair was perfectly smooth. Not a hair out of place.

I couldn't resist. "How's it going?" I said. I reached out and mussed up her hair. You know. Just being friendly.

Her green eyes went wide. Her mouth formed an O of surprise.

And then I uttered a cry. Staring down, I saw that a chunk of her hair had come off in my hand!

A thick tuft of her brown hair was twined in my fingers. She had a bald spot on top of her head. She grabbed her head and backed away from me.

"No! No way!" I cried.

A crowd quickly gathered around me. The kids' faces were cold. Not friendly. "Hey, guys," I said. "I'm the new kid. This looks like an awesome school."

A skinny kid with spiky blond hair stood with his hands on his waist, watching me with narrowed black eyes. "Yo. What's up?" I said. I reached out and bumped knuckles with him.

Uh-oh.

His hand came off with a soft ripping sound, and it fell to the floor with a *splat*.

A gasp escaped my throat. I stared at the hand down on the floor.

"Uh . . . sorry about that," I said.

The crowd had grown bigger and uglier. It was easy to see that I'd made a bad first impression. These kids didn't like me.

I sighed. I felt so disappointed. I really wanted to have a fresh start here. Make some new friends.

But these kids were coming apart. I mean, their hair and hands were falling off. How creepy is that?

"What's up with this school?" I said. "Where do you all come from?"

No one answered.

A big, fat-faced kid with tiny bird eyes on a broad nose, and straight blond hair falling over his wide forehead, bumped up to me. I saw that his hands were curled into fists. I knew instantly that he wasn't coming over to welcome me. This guy was trouble.

I stood my ground. I stared into his little bird eyes. "Would you like a dance lesson?" I said.

I didn't wait for his answer. I raised my shoe—and stomped down as hard as I could on top of his left foot.

You'll never guess what he did.

Nothing.

He didn't do anything.

He stood perfectly still. As if it didn't hurt him at all. As if he didn't even notice that I'd pounded his foot into the floor.

I tried again. I gave him another dance lesson. I tromped as hard as I could on his right foot.

"Nothing. Nada. Zilch. Zip," as the Ghost of Christmas Future would say.

He stood there, hulking over me, his fists curling and uncurling. A low moan rose up from the crowd of kids. They didn't speak. They only moaned. They had formed a circle and were closing in on me.

What did they plan to do?

I didn't wait to find out. I ducked my head and burst between two girls, shoving them out of my way. My shoes pounded the hard floor as I ran toward the front of the school.

Their frightening moans followed me. I didn't turn back. I shoved open the heavy double doors and burst outside. The moans cut off as the doors shut behind me.

I took off running. I ran to the side of the building and turned the corner. The black tower rose above me. I ran in its shadow. My heart pounded. My legs trembled as if they were made of Jell-O.

The air felt cold against my burning face. Over the thud of my footsteps, I heard the harsh squawks of the vultures high overhead.

I followed the black stone wall. It led to a wide courtyard behind the school. I stopped when I saw the gravestones.

"Whoa."

Gravestones? Behind a school?

They were in neat rows. Low granite stones with rounded tops. All the same size, all tilting straight up in the tall grass of the courtyard.

A loud screech made me jump. Did the sound come

from a grave? No. A black cat darted between the rows of graves, its tail held stiffly high.

I glanced back. No one had followed me. I was all alone in this strange school cemetery.

The wind made a shrill whistling sound as it blew through the gravestones. And the ugly squawk of the vultures overhead never stopped.

I stepped closer. Close enough to read the names engraved on the stones. Of course, I didn't recognize any of them.

But I gasped when I read the dates engraved beneath the names. The kids buried here had all died at age ten or eleven or twelve.

A shiver rolled down my body. A cemetery of kids' graves . . . Dead Middle School . . . Those silent kids I met in the hall with their hair falling off and hands dropping to the floor.

Zombies!

I don't know why it took me so long to put it together. But I finally realized the kids I met in that hallway were all dead. Zombies. Were they buried here in this little graveyard? Probably.

The Ghost of Christmas Future had dropped me off in a school of zombie kids. *"This is where you belong, Scroogeman."* That's what he had said.

"This is where you belong."

And as I walked along the row of low graves, my whole body shook in shudder after shudder. Was I stuck here with these zombies forever?

I stopped suddenly. My breath caught in my throat. My knees started to buckle. I nearly fell into the open grave in front of me.

A fresh, open hole, a deep rectangle cut into the earth. An open grave.

My eyes bulged and I let out a loud gasp as I read the name engraved on the stone: RICK SCROOGEMAN.

So the robot Ghost of the Future really did plan to leave me here forever. He really had given up on me.

But that wasn't fair. Not fair at all.

I stumbled back. I wanted to get away from the terrifying gravestone. But something held me there. Something stopped me from turning around and running.

I heard a whisper. It seemed to come from down in the open grave.

"Come downnnnnnn."

No. I imagined that. In my fright, my brain was playing tricks on me.

"Come downnnn."

"No!" I cried out loud. "I'm not hearing this! Stop! I don't hear it!"

"*Come downnnn, Scroogeman.*"

And then I saw a dim flash of movement. Just a blur of gray at the bottom of the hole.

I couldn't help myself. I was too terrified to run. Too terrified to move. But I leaned forward. Leaned over the grave to see what was moving down there.

I opened my mouth to scream when I saw them. But no sound came out.

I stared down at the kids in the grave. They were crowded in there. At least a dozen of them. All staring up at me.

I recognized a few of them from inside the school. I saw the girl with the perfect hair. And the big guy with the bird eyes, the guy I gave a dancing lesson.

I tried to choke out another scream, but I couldn't catch my breath. They were huddled in my grave—and I could see right through them! They were transparent, all in shades of gray. No color.

No color because they were dead!

And now they raised their arms. All at once, they shot their arms up out of the hole. Hands wrapped around my feet. Two guys floated up and wrapped their arms around my waist.

"Nooooo!" I finally found my voice, and a howl of horror burst from my throat. "Noooo! Let GO of me!"

But they started to tug me down, down into the grave. A hum of excitement rose from down in the hole. They were all humming, humming a single note. Singing me to my grave.

I struggled with all my strength. But the hands tightened around my ankles with surprising strength. And more hands wrapped around my legs and waist.

The humming grew louder as the hands pulled and my shoes scraped the dirt at the edge of the hole. Then I started to sink. They were lowering me into the grave, humming, eyes wide, staring without blinking. Eyes wide and blank as they pulled me down.

I opened my mouth and screamed again—in a pleading cracked voice I didn't recognize: "No, please! Please! I'm not dead! I'm not dead! I don't want to be a zombie! Please let me goooooo!"

28

As I started to slide down the dirt, down the front of the grave, I swung my body hard. I heard a ripping sound. One of the arms holding my waist fell off. The arm ripped off at the shoulder and fell to the dirt.

I kicked at the hands gripping my shoes. Kicked hard. Again. Again.

The hands went flying.

I frantically ripped away arms and hands. The humming stopped. The only sound now was the whistle of the wind through the graves and the squawk of the vultures circling overhead.

With a groan, I spun around and grabbed the soft dirt at the side of the grave with both hands. I don't know where I found the strength. I guess it came from my total terror. I scrambled up to the surface, my shoes kicking and sliding on the steep side of the grave.

I climbed up to the ground and glanced back down. The dead kids were bent over, recovering their hands and arms. Some dead kids had picked up the wrong hands and were passing them to their owners.

I forced myself to turn away and, sucking in a deep, shuddering breath, I started to run. I didn't know where to run. I just knew I had to get away from the dead kids and their frightening school as fast as I could.

My shoes pounded the grass. I watched the red sun lowering itself behind a row of tall, leafy trees ahead of me. I passed wide grassy lots and then came to a block of small, redbrick houses.

I didn't stop. My side ached and my chest burned, but I kept running. And I didn't look back.

Where was I? Was I really in the future? In the year 2095?

Was there any way I'd ever find my way back to my home, to my mom and brother, back in the time I belonged?

I tried to force these questions from my mind as I

ran. I wanted to concentrate on getting as far away from the dead school as I could.

Would the Ghost of Christmas Future find me and drag me back there?

That was another question I didn't want to think about.

I turned a corner and found myself on a block of larger houses, all very neat, with closely trimmed lawns and shrubs, and tall hedges along the curb.

I saw kids playing with some kind of radio-controlled flying drone. It flew very high and they chased after it, arms outstretched to catch it. At the end of the block, a man was showing a little girl how to ride a bike, running alongside her as she pedaled.

Normal life.

For a moment, I thought maybe I had run back to my time. But the bike had some kind of jets on the back. And the cars in the driveways were all silver and shaped like rocket ships.

Suddenly, I had an idea.

I stopped running. My legs felt as if they weighed a thousand pounds each. My chest felt about to explode.

Some kids were soaring toward me on some kind of power skates. I ducked behind a tall shrub, lowered my hands to my knees, and struggled to catch my breath.

My idea would have to wait till night, I decided. It was a crazy idea. An impossible idea. But I couldn't have been more desperate.

I had come so close to death. I had just escaped from my own grave. I knew I had to try *anything* to get away from here. I never cry. I never cried even when I was a baby. I told you before. I'm just not the kind of guy who likes to cry.

But every time I thought about Charlie and my mom, celebrating Christmas without me . . . Every time I thought about how far away they were, and how I probably would never see them again . . . my eyes watered and my chin started to quiver. And I had to grit my teeth and force myself not to give in . . . not to cry.

Hiding behind the tall shrub, I thought hard about a lot of things. I never realized how important Mom and Charlie were to me. I just never thought about that.

And I never realized how much I really wanted friends. I wanted Lucy Copperfield and Davey Pittman and Josh Cratchit to be my friends. I wanted them to like me, not hate me.

"If I ever get back home, I'll never make fun of Josh's stutter again," I told myself. "And I'll never mess up Lucy's hair or give Davey dancing lessons."

I was sincere. I wasn't just saying that. I was willing to change my whole personality. Just to get back.

I peered around the side of the bush and watched the house at the top of the lawn. Through the front window, I could see a large video screen. It appeared to stretch over a whole wall.

In the glare of the screen, I saw a boy and a girl sitting on opposite ends of a shiny, silver couch. They were watching some kind of animated show with strange animal warriors fighting with laser weapons.

I stuck my head out a little farther. Gazing into the window, I saw a woman pull the two kids from the couch. The screen went blank. I guessed it was the family dinnertime.

I pulled back behind the bush and sat down on the lawn. It wasn't grass. It was some kind of springy, rubbery stuff I'd never seen before. I realized the bush wasn't real, either. It was made of that same rubbery stuff. The lawn and bushes of the future?

I settled my back against the bush and concentrated on my plan. I ignored my rumbling stomach. When was the last time I had eaten?

I knew I couldn't start until the family had gone to bed. That would be hours from now. But the wait would be worth it—if my idea worked.

I yawned. I suddenly felt exhausted. I guess it was all the fright . . . the dead kids . . . the open grave . . . running for my life. That would make *anyone* tired.

I shut my eyes and immediately fell asleep. When I woke up, it was dark out, no moon or stars in the sky. I peered down the street. No one around. No cars—or whatever they drove in 2095—passing by.

The lights were off in most of the houses I could see. I didn't know what time it was, but I guessed it was pretty late. I reached my arms above my head and tried to stretch the stiffness from my back.

I pulled myself onto my knees and peered up at the house. The big video screen was blank. The lights were all off. Time for me to make my move.

Was I really doing this?

Was I really breaking into this house?

Yes.

I found a half-open window on the side wall. I pulled myself up onto the window ledge and slowly, carefully slid the window up, wide enough for me to climb inside.

Silently, I lowered myself into the house. My shoes

made a soft thud on a deep, shaggy carpet. I was at the back of the living room. The big video screen stood to my left. Turning right, I saw the family Christmas tree, metallic silver, glistening even in the dark.

The house smelled of roast chicken. My stomach grumbled again. I thought of creeping into the kitchen and helping myself to a little dinner.

But I didn't want to delay. I was eager to see if I stood any chance at all of my plan working.

My eyes slowly adjusted to the darkness. The living room was filled with sleek, shiny furniture. It all gleamed like metal, even in the dim light.

I saw two dark doorways against the far wall. I took a few careful steps toward them. I wanted to stay away from the family bedrooms where they were all sleeping. I stood there trying to decide which hallway to try.

My heart was pounding hard. I could feel the blood pulsing at my temples. I suddenly realized this was a terrible idea. Frightening thoughts whirred through my brain.

What if they wake up? What if they think I am a burglar? What if they have some kind of gun and shoot me before I have a chance to explain?

And . . .

How could I ever explain this?

The plan seemed worth a try when it first came to me. After all, my ghost troubles had all started in a closet. When the first ghost appeared, I was in the attic closet in my house where all the Christmas presents for Charlie and me were hidden.

The Ghost of Christmas Past. That's what he called himself. He appeared in the closet and took me away, took me to the past and that horrible school.

So here's what I thought.

Maybe a *closet* was the way to travel back home. Maybe if I hid in a closet—a closet I didn't belong in—I would be carried away again. Carried back to my time and to my mom and little brother.

Standing there in the dark house staring at the two hallways, I knew it was a crazy idea. Totally insane. Doomed to failure.

But I didn't have any other ideas. I was alone and afraid and lost.

So can you blame me? I *had* to try the closet idea.

I crept into the hall to the left. I was walking on tiptoe, one step at a time, holding my breath, trying not to make a sound. I squinted down the long hall, searching for a closet door.

Suddenly, a door opened right behind me. I slammed

my hand over my mouth to keep from crying out. I pressed myself as tightly against the wall as I could and watched as a short figure stepped out into the hallway.

I recognized him. The boy I had seen through the front window. The boy watching the animated film on the big screen.

I started to choke. I felt as if my heart had leapt into my mouth. I held my breath and pressed myself into the deep shadow of the wall.

Please don't see me. Please don't see me.

The boy turned away from me and walked toward the kitchen. His bare feet slapped the hard floor. A few seconds later, I heard water running. He was getting a drink in the kitchen.

I knew he'd be back in the hall in a few seconds. And this time he'd definitely see me because he'd be facing me.

I fought off the wave of panic that froze my body. Spun away from the wall. Darted to the next door— and pulled it open.

29

I stared into solid blackness. Was this a closet? I couldn't see for sure. But I had no choice. I ducked inside and pulled the door shut behind me.

Gasping for breath, my chest heaving up and down, I stood there for a long moment, just trying to get myself together.

Hey, you *know* I'm not a scaredy-cat. I'm a pretty bold guy. But I wasn't cut out to be a burglar. I had no idea what they did to people who broke into houses in the future, but it couldn't be good.

Finally, I started to breathe normally. My heart slid back down to my chest. I fumbled on the wall and found a light switch. I clicked it on, and a pale yellow ceiling light flashed on.

I blinked. The light hurt my eyes. I gazed around. Yes. I was in a long, narrow closet.

It was a supply closet. Against the back wall I saw colorful boxes and bottles of cleaning supplies. The closet floor was cluttered with tools and appliances. I couldn't recognize most of them. Was that a vacuum cleaner? It looked like a small car!

Pressing my ear against the closet door, I heard the slap of the boy's bare feet in the hall. I heard him walk back into his room and click the door shut.

Good. I was all alone now. Alone in a closet.

I dropped to the floor, sat down, put my hands on my knees, and pressed my back against the closet wall. Now what? What do I do? How do I summon a ghost to take me home?

I suddenly felt stupid. *I'm sitting in a closet in a house I don't belong in and I don't have a clue.*

Was there some way to call a ghost?

Was there any chance at all that this closet could lead me back to my closet at home? Even a million-to-one chance?

I had to try it. I decided to shut my eyes and wish. Yes. Wish for a Christmas ghost to carry me back home.

Sometimes wishes come true, don't they?

I shut my eyes and hugged my knees. I thought about the three ghosts and how they wanted to teach me lessons. How they wanted me to change.

Well, I WILL change, I told myself. *I can be kind. And I can be generous. And I can really mean it, not just think it.*

Those were my thoughts, sitting there so frightened and so desperate in that closet.

I kept my eyes shut and my head down. And I wished . . . and wished . . . and silently wished.

And nothing happened.

30

Nothing happened for about ten minutes.

And then I felt a puff of cold wind. I opened my eyes in time to see the closet fill with a purple light. The light grew brighter . . . brighter . . . until I had to shield my eyes.

The closet began to shake. The shelves rattled. The bottles and boxes tilted and fell. Like an earthquake, the floor rose up in a roar, then fell. I was tossed forward onto my stomach.

And as I scrambled to stand up, the floor beneath me vanished. The whole closet disappeared. And I was floating on a thick purple carpet of air.

I toppled over and over as I flew, tossed one way,

then the other, as if caught in an invisible swirling tornado.

Was that *me* screaming?

Yes. My mouth was open in an endless howl of horror. I was flying out of control, swirling and swerving, climbing and dipping. My arms flailed helplessly at my sides. My feet thrashed the air. And all I could see was that deep violet color, so thick I could almost taste it.

How long did I fly like that? How long did I scream? My throat was raw and throbbing. My face felt burned from the wind.

I landed hard. Landed in a heap. My elbows banged a solid wood floor, my head bumped a wall, and pain shot down my whole body.

I forced myself to stand up. My mouth hung open. I could still hear the roar of the purple wind in my ears. Sucking in air, I glanced around. I knew instantly where I was.

I was home.

I gazed at the stack of Christmas presents, their wrapping all ripped and ruined.

"I'm back in the attic closet!" I told myself. Yes. Everything still here, just as I left it. Charlie's presents ripped open. My presents strewn on the floor where I left them . . .

"I'm back! It worked! It worked!" I cried, pumping my fists in the air.

I lowered my shoulder and shoved open the closet door. I burst into the attic. I darted to the stairs and flew down them two at a time.

Was this the happiest moment of my life? You don't have to ask.

Home. Back home. Here I was. It even *smelled* like home.

I stumbled and nearly fell over as I reached the bottom of the stairs. I was so eager to see Mom and Charlie, I felt as if my whole body was about to burst—like a balloon.

"Mom! I'm home!" I screamed breathlessly. "Mom? Charlie?"

My shoes thudded down the hall as I ran shouting all the way. I passed the kitchen. I saw an uneaten roast turkey on a platter on the counter. Several other dishes of delicious-looking food.

"Mom? Charlie?"

They weren't in the kitchen. I turned and darted into the front hallway. Yes! I saw them. I saw them in the living room. Charlie was sprawled on his stomach on the floor, a book in his hands. Mom sat on the tall green armchair, tapping her fingers on the chair arms, a pile of knitting on her lap.

"Hey, it's me!" I cried. "Were you worried about me? Mom? Charlie? Here I am!"

Why didn't they turn around? I was screaming at the top of my lungs.

Why didn't they hear me?

Charlie turned the page of the book he was reading. He didn't look up.

Mom picked up her knitting needles and said something to him. I couldn't hear her. Charlie nodded.

"Hey—here I am!" I shouted. "Mom! Charlie! I'm home!"

They didn't turn around.

A sob escaped my throat. This was *too weird*.

I was standing in the wide entryway to the living room. I raised my arms, eager to hug Mom. I took a step toward her—and gasped in shock.

Something held me back.

I tried to move forward again. But something—an invisible wall—kept me from Mom and Charlie. Something pushed me back, blocked my way into the living room.

"Mom? Charlie?" My cry came out shrill and trembling. "Help me. Please. I'm here. Can't you see me?"

Charlie yawned and turned another page in his book. Mom settled back in her chair and started to knit.

31

I lowered my shoulder and pushed it against the invisible barrier. I couldn't budge it. I strained and struggled, pushing the invisible wall with all my might.

"That won't do you any good, Scroogeman," a voice said.

I spun around and gasped again. I stared at the Ghost of Christmas Present. Stared at his bulby nose and red cheeks, his ringlets of curly orange hair beneath his tall shiny black top hat. He wore the same red bow tie and still had a matching red flower in the lapel of his checkered jacket.

"Why not?" I cried. "Why can't they see me or hear me? Why can't I go to them?"

"You cannot go back to your life, Scrooge," the

ghost said, shaking his head. "Not until you prove you are ready."

"I'm ready," I said. "I've changed. I'm a totally new person! I'm kind now. I'm generous. I'm going to be nice to everyone. You have to let me back to my family. I miss them *so much*."

The ghost frowned at me. "We Christmas ghosts don't do this for our health, Scroogeman. We took you away because you were ruining Christmas for everyone."

"I know. I know. But that's the past—" I insisted. "That's before I learned what my friends really think of me. Before I learned how horrible I was."

"You have to prove it," he said. "I can't just take your word for it. You have to prove that you've changed."

"No problem," I said. "I *will* prove it. I want to. I want to show everyone that I'm a new Rick Scroogeman."

He fiddled with his bow tie. "Well . . . go ahead. Show me that you have changed. And I'll send you back to your family in time for Christmas."

"And my birthday," I said. "Don't forget my birthday."

But he had vanished once again. Ghosts have a

habit of disappearing while you're still talking to them. It's very rude—but I wasn't about to complain.

The aroma of the roast turkey filled my nostrils. I saw Mom and Charlie in the next room, so close and yet so far away. Once again, I had a sudden urge to cry. Can you imagine?

That's how desperate I was to get back, to be with Mom and Charlie and have a real Christmas.

I suddenly had a plan. I knew just what I wanted to do.

I started with Lucy Copperfield. I walked through tall snowdrifts to her house in the next block.

Was the Ghost of Christmas Present watching me?

I didn't care. I didn't need him there. I knew what I had to do.

I kicked snow off my shoes as I stepped onto Lucy's front stoop. I rang the doorbell. After a few seconds, a voice shouted, "Go away!" It was Lucy.

"I just came to talk to you," I shouted through the door.

"Go away, Rick," she repeated. The door opened a crack. I could see one of her eyes peering out at me. "I know what you're going to do," she said. "You're going to smear my glasses with your thumbs. Then you're going to mess up my hair."

"No. No way," I said. "Open the door, Lucy. I came to wish you a Merry Christmas."

"Ha!" she exclaimed. "Double ha. I heard your essay in Miss Dorrit's class, remember? 'Bah, Humbug. Why I hate Christmas'? Everyone heard what you wrote, Rick."

"No. That was a long time ago," I said. "I was wrong. That essay was wrong. I've changed, Lucy, and—"

"Beat it, Rick," she snapped. "I'm working on an art project and I don't want it to dry."

"I can help you with it," I said. "I'm a good artist. Let me help you. Please."

"Ha!" she repeated. It seemed to be her word of the day.

"I can help you with your homework," I said. "Would you like that? Or I could walk Hank for you. I know you hate walking your dog in the snow. Let me walk Hank."

"Stop trying to trick me, Rick," she said.

"Would you like to bake cookies together?" I said. "We could have fun making Christmas cookies. Seriously."

"And you'll smear cookie dough in my face?"

"No. No way. We can make little stars and little Christmas trees and—"

BANG. She slammed the door hard in my face. I nearly toppled off the stoop.

"Lucy?" I called through the door. "Come back. I just want to be your friend."

Silence. She didn't return.

I sighed and slumped away.

Josh Cratchit lived in a tiny brick house two blocks away. I trudged through the snow and rang his bell. His mom opened the door. She seemed very surprised to see me.

I stepped inside. They had a scrawny Christmas tree in one corner. It was nearly bare. I didn't see any presents under the tree. Josh's baby brother was wailing his head off in a highchair. Josh's twin sisters were trying to quiet the baby.

"Josh is in his room," his mom said, pointing to the door. "Does he know you're coming over?"

"It's a surprise," I said. I poked my head into Josh's room. "Merry Christmas," I said, flashing him a friendly smile.

"D-d-don't HURT me!" he cried. He jumped up from behind his laptop and backed away, holding both arms in front of him like a shield. "Please, Rick—don't h-h-h-hurt me!"

"I just came over to say hi to a good friend," I said. I raised my hand and stepped toward him. "Give me five, friend!"

"N-n-no. Please!" he begged. "Please don't p-p-p-punch me in the stomach or give me a wedgie or p-p-pull my shirt out from my jeans or twist my arm behind my b-b-back till it cracks."

I shook my head. "Would I do something like that? That was the old Rick Scroogeman. Now I'm different. I came over to be your friend." I pointed. "Look. Your sneakers are untied. Let me tie them for you. And I see that pile of dirty laundry on the floor. Let me do your laundry for you, okay? I can do all your chores, Josh. Like a real friend. Wouldn't that be awesome?"

"G-g-go away," Josh replied. He backed all the way against the wall. His eyes were wide with fright. "Please, Rick. Give me a b-b-break. I know you're going to hurt m-m-m-me. Go away!"

I suddenly had a heavy feeling of dread in the pit of my stomach. No one believed that I had changed. Did this mean I'd never be able to return to my family?

My shoulders slumped in defeat, I crept out of the

house. I could still hear Josh's baby brother crying. The sun had disappeared behind heavy clouds. The air had become cold and raw.

Where should I try next? I didn't have a clue.

And then suddenly, I had a great idea.

32

I hurried home. My brain was spinning. My plan had to work. I *had* to get back to Mom and Charlie. I was desperate to be home with them for Christmas.

I didn't want to think about what would happen to me if I failed again.

Mom and Charlie were in the kitchen. Mom was setting the kitchen table. Charlie was chewing on a Fruit Roll-Up, his favorite kind of fruit.

I called to them and tried to step into the kitchen. But the invisible wall blocked my way. They couldn't hear or see me.

A wave of sadness swept over me. I fought it off. I still had hope. I knew I had one more chance.

I climbed the steep steps to the attic and made my

way quickly to the closet. I clicked on the light. The presents I had greedily unwrapped were still strewn on the closet floor.

I searched frantically through the presents until I found the ones I wanted to give away. I struggled to rewrap them as best as I could. Then I hurried back out of the house, into the snow and biting, cold air and the cloudy charcoal sky.

Back on Lucy's stoop, my finger trembled as I rang the bell.

"Go away!" I heard her angry shout inside the house. "I told you to beat it, Scroogeman!"

"But . . . but . . . ," I sputtered. "Lucy, I brought you two Christmas presents."

I held my breath. Would she open the door?

Yes. She pulled it open halfway and eyed the packages in my hands suspiciously. "Is this one of your tricks?"

I pushed the two presents into her hands. "No. Merry Christmas, Lucy. These are for you. I picked them out special. I hope you like them."

She still had that suspicious look on her face. She opened the first one. "What is this?" she demanded. "Handkerchiefs?"

I nodded. "They are for wiping your glasses clean whenever I smear them with my thumbs," I said.

That brought a smile to her face. "Seriously?"

"Yes," I said. "Open the other present."

She opened it and stared at the present I'd given her. "Huh? A hairbrush?"

"That's for when I mess up your hair," I said. "You'll always be ready to brush it again."

Lucy laughed. "That's awesome. Great gifts, Rick. At least, I know they'll come in handy." Her expression changed. "Sorry I didn't get you a present."

"No problem," I replied. "I just want you to be my friend." I stared at her. "Will you be my friend?"

A long pause. Finally, she said, "Okay. We can give it a try."

She stepped back. "Do you want to come in? We could work on my art project together."

"Maybe later," I said. "That would be awesome. But I have another present to give out. See you later."

As I made my way down her snowy front yard, my heart started to pound a little harder. This next one was going to be harder.

A lot harder.

33

A few minutes later, I stepped up to Josh Cratchit's house. The baby had stopped crying. But now Josh's twin sisters were fighting—screaming and yelling. Something about which one of them broke an American Girl doll.

Josh lives in a very noisy house. I understood why he liked to shut himself up in his room.

When I poked my head into his room, he jumped up again. His face went pale and he staggered back to the wall. "Wh-what do you want?" he stammered, his eyes wide with fear.

I handed him the present I'd brought from my closet. "Here," I said. "This is for you, Josh. Merry Christmas."

He eyed me suspiciously, the same expression Lucy had. He unwrapped the present and stared at it. "A s-songbook? *A Christmas Carol* s-s-songbook?"

I nodded. "Yes. For you."

"B-b-but why?" he demanded.

"A few weeks ago, I saw this show on Nickelodeon," I explained. "It was about kids who stutter. And one kid said that he stuttered when he talked, but he *never* stuttered when he *sang.* And I thought maybe you'd like to try it. Maybe singing will help you."

Josh's mouth dropped open. He gaped at me wide-eyed. "Rick, what a n-n-nice gift," he said. "You really w-wanted to help me?"

"Yes," I said. "And, Josh, I promise I'll never make fun of you again."

He stared at me, trying to figure out if I was serious.

"Let's try it," I said. I took the book from his hands and opened it to the first song. "Silent Night."

Josh hesitated. "I d-d-don't know. I—"

"Come on. We'll sing it together," I said. I held the book between us and started to sing. We both sang "Silent Night," and it sounded pretty good. And Josh didn't stutter. Not once.

"Let's try another one," I said.

I turned the page and we sang "It Came Upon a Midnight Clear." And again, Josh didn't stutter once.

When we finished the song, he had tears in his eyes. He shook hands with me. He actually *shook hands*. "Rick, this is the n-n-nicest present I ever got," he said.

"I hope that means we can be friends," I said.

He shook my hand again. "Friends."

I felt so good as I left Josh's house, I hopped down the porch stairs and did a cartwheel in the snow. When I stood up, the Ghost of Christmas Present was standing there.

He flashed me a thumbs-up. "Go home, Scroogeman," he said. "It's almost Christmas."

I RAN INTO THE KITCHEN, WRAPPED MY ARMS AROUND MOM'S waist and hugged her tight. "I'm home. I'm home, Mom," I choked out.

I kissed her cheek. I hugged her again. Then I gave Charlie a long, tight hug. My throat felt choked with emotion. I couldn't speak. Couldn't make a sound.

"Rick, where have you been?" Mom asked. "You've been gone nearly an hour."

An hour? That's all?

"Uh . . . I went to see Lucy and Josh," I said.

"Well, sit down," Mom said. "I knew you wouldn't be late for Christmas Eve dinner. And, hey, it's almost your birthday. I have your favorite cake."

"That's nice," I said. "But I'm just so happy to be here, to spend Christmas and my birthday with you and Charlie. My awesome family."

Mom squinted at me. "Rick? Do you have a fever or something? You're acting weird. Are you okay?"

"Yes," I said. "I'm just so excited to be back and—"

"Well, sit down and stop yammering," Mom said. "The food is getting cold."

And so . . .

It started out as the worst, most frightening Christmas ever. But it ended up as the best Christmas and birthday I ever had.

My new attitude changed everything. I loved all my presents. I loved my birthday cake, although vanilla isn't my favorite. I loved playing video games with Charlie. I even shared my birthday candy with him.

Because of my frightening adventures, because of the three ghosts and the horror they put me through, I was a changed kid. I was bubbling with happiness. And I loved Christmas. Everything about it.

I couldn't wait to get back to school after New Year's to show everyone the new Rick Scroogeman.

That morning, I wore a new pair of straight-leg jeans and the red-and-black ski sweater Mom had knitted for me for Christmas. I felt good and I wanted to look good.

And wouldn't you know it as I walked down the hall for the first time in the New Year, there was Davey Pittman bending over the water fountain. "Yo, Davey!" I called.

I couldn't resist. I cupped my hands in the fountain, filled them with water, and sent a big splash to the front of Davey's jeans. Ha-ha.

Hey—no one is perfect.